Chapter 1: This Can't Happening... but it is.

Sarah Aston awoke with a banging headache.

"Why oh why did I drink wine last night" she whispered to herself.

Her husband Mike lay still asleep beside her. She ignored him as she put her bathrobe on and headed to the bathroom to splash water over her face. It never works to freshen her up but she does it anyway like a ritual.

This is the third or fourth morning in a row that Sarah has felt hung over. And it pops into Sarah's mind that she doesn't think she is drinking too much. In the past she could have had nine or ten large glasses and still felt fresh as a daisy the next morning. And yet here we are... feeling hung over from just five. Maybe it's something else she thought to herself.

Sarah's cell phone rings. It's Lara Hine, an imaginative 36 year old who writes short stories for a living. And she's Sarah's best friend. Sarah tells her she is feeling like shit.

"Well, it's the perfect excuse to decline sex with your husband" says Lara. Lara is the only person who could normally get away with such a statement. But Sarah is fast falling out of love with Mike. So maybe now, she would allow almost anyone to say such a thing.

"That's funny" replied Sarah.

"I will need you drinking less wine so you'll do it with me" added Lara laughing. Lara was laughing so as to cast doubt in Sarah's mind over whether or not she was being serious. But Lara was being serious. She had been wanting to take things further with her best friend for months and Sarah slanted heavily in her thinking that this was the case.

"Hey Lara, I am a psychiatrist you know… so I can read your mind. I will prove it. You are 36 years old".

"If you could read my mind, you would have hung up the phone given the things I am imagining right now" replied Lara, again laughing as she said it. "Anyway, I will see you after work, we can grab a coffee"

Sarah hung up the phone and felt very strong cognitive dissonance over her friendship. And who could blame her after that phone call.

"She's deliberately doing this… attempting to get me to go along with this change in our friendship" said Sarah out-loud to herself.

And yet, she felt more anxiety still over her relationship with her husband. But the two issues were becoming inextricably linked. And that phone call was too much. Annoyed at the forwardness of her friend, and still feeling physically like shit she locked herself in the bathroom. And suddenly to make things worse she experienced flickering's of an absolutely terrifying nightmare last night.

I can't handle a bit of wine, my boring book store owning husband bores me, and my best friend is harassing me. Oh and my unconscious is deciding to contribute its part… the straw that broke the camel's back part in the Holy Grail quest to make Sarah Aston go insane.

So this is light years away from the best mind-state for a psychiatrist to be in.

And I've got to go to work.

As Sarah got ready for work she was thinking more about the discussion she was going to have with Lara over that coffee more than she was thinking about any relationship problems of her analysand's… a term that her psychiatrist colleagues hated her using because it derives from Freud and psychoanalysis. But Sarah was close to psychoanalysis in some regards.

Why not just cancel all my sessions for today and just see myself, Sarah Aston. Afterall, she seems most in-need of some frigging therapy!

Sarah works as a psychiatrist at the Boston Mental Health Institute, a facility providing comprehensive mental health services to patients in Boston and the surrounding areas.

The institute is a large, modern facility located in the heart of the city, with state-of-the-art equipment and highly trained staff.

A typical day for Sarah at the Boston Mental Health Institute begins with her arriving at the facility early in the morning. She checks her schedule for the day and reviews notes from previous sessions with her patients. Sarah sees patients throughout the day, conducting individual therapy sessions, group therapy sessions, and medication management appointments. She works with a wide range of patients, including those struggling with anxiety, depression, bipolar disorder, schizophrenia, and other mental health conditions.

During her individual therapy sessions, Sarah listens carefully to her patients' concerns and works with them to develop treatment plans tailored to their specific needs. While most of her colleagues use evidence-based therapies such as cognitive-behavioral therapy (CBT), dialectical behavior therapy (DBT), Sarah leans more to psychoanalytical ideas although she is no slave to Freud. She has the same end goal as her colleagues which is to help her patients manage their symptoms and improve their overall quality of life.

In addition to her individual therapy sessions, Sarah also leads group therapy sessions for patients with similar mental health concerns. These sessions provide a supportive environment where patients can share their experiences and learn from one another.

Throughout the day, Sarah also meets with other members of the mental health team at the Boston Mental Health Institute. She consults with psychiatrists, psychologists, social workers, and other healthcare professionals to ensure that her patients receive comprehensive care.

At the end of a long day of seeing patients and collaborating with colleagues, Sarah takes some time to complete paperwork and update patient records before heading home.

Overall, Sarah's work as a psychiatrist at the Boston Mental Health Institute is challenging but rewarding. She is able to make a real difference in the lives of her patients by providing them with compassionate care. Except when Sarah is having an off-day like she is today. Then her work becomes an additional problem.

Sarah's first analysand today was Richard. Richard seemingly wasted no time in stating his problem.

"I have been having terrifying and recurring nightmares of alien abduction. I am asleep in my bed when suddenly I dream of waking to a buzzing or humming sound in my ears. Then all of a sudden it's like it's gone from pitch black outside to a glorious summers day with sunshine that makes you squint your eyes. And then… ". Richard stopped in his tracks.

"Go on" encourages Sarah as she sees Richard struggle with the memories making Sarah think this is surely a highly imaginative person, too imaginative, because she's already certain that the PTSD is real. In the back of Sarah's mind is her own recent encounter with the unconscsious which is nagging away at her now but she temporarily relatively manages to repress those thoughts and memories.

Richard's voice became more anxious, loud and fast in tone as he says "Then there are these little guys, grey, they just materialize in my bedroom. I put off getting help for so long because I thought no one would believe me. You do believe me right?"

"I believe you are having these experiences and they are traumatic for you, of course. You said they were nightmares but I am thinking you are trying to tell me that you think they are much more than just nightmares?"

"They levitate me AND I DON'T KNOW HOW THEY DO IT. We enter a craft by going through solid walls AND I DON'T KNOW HOW THEY MAKE THAT HAPPEN!"

Sarah feels empathy. It's what makes her a good psychiatrist on most days.

"It's ok. It's ok. I believe you".

"NO YOU DON'T. YOU THINK ITS ALL IN MY HEAD!"

"Look, Richard. I know it's a coincidence but I have had similar nightmares recently. Even last night".

"You are getting ABDUCTED??" Richard meant that response literally and Sarah knows he did, making her pause to try and answer in a way that isn't a Yes but isn't breaking the empathy she is trying to express.

"I think it's more than just a normal nightmare. I think it's archetypal. A collective dream that we are all capable of experiencing and that almost all of us think is impossible until we do experience it. Humans are more imaginative than we think we are. This amazing imagination is not conscious to us. We do not think we are capable of it but it's in all of us, even two year old toddlers can experience what we are going through".

Sarah's Jungian style answer is met with a "huh?" from Richard. He doesn't want to sound dumb and more importantly to him he is wondering whether or not this means she thinks it's real or not? But she has him feeling more confused than empathised with.

"This feels real. Very real! As real as this! More real than this! Much more real tha….."

Sarah interrupts. "Yes. That is how it is supposed to be experienced. It is 100 per cent psychologically real".

Richard doesn't like the response. "No. It's physically real. I can touch things. I can even smell the greys. They have a distinctive smell".

Sarah still flustered from her own life, is beginning to remember more of her own nightmares. She gets a flash of a grey and it feels like a memory of something that happened when awake. She suddenly reacts to seemingly nothing with a look of concern. It's enough for Richard to ask if she is alright?

"Yes. Yes. As I said a moment ago, I too have been having nightmares".

"Maybe you are being abducted Sarah".

Sarah became unprofessional for a moment with her thoughts. Normally she would ensure that anything she said would be expressed empathically and sometimes just listening and encouraging openness would be enough for her. But now she reacted more like she would if chatting with a friend in a bar or coffee shop.

"Oh I just think that what is happening to us Richard is something along the lines of what Carl Jung and his friend Pauli would have said. Reality is psychophysical deep down and yeah, this surprises me too. I prefer Freud. But when you hear about experiences like this and NDE's, well they can't all be denied. But it doesn't mean they are literally happening. Believe me, you are NOT literally getting abducted by aliens. Sleep paralysis has to be suspected of playing a part to. You know, people have had these experiences for millennia. Grey aliens fit with our time."

Richard found Sarah's little speech intolerable especially as she expressed what she just said in a dismissive tone of voice. He did not feel empathised with at all, he felt like she had been inconsiderate and failing to understand. He now thought of her as unhelpful. He got out of his chair and stood up. He walked over to a seated Sarah and looked down at her, pointed his finger at her and said

"Maybe you are just having nightmares. But what I am experiencing is f*****g real. It's not me that is living in Wonderland. It's you!" With that Richard stormed out, not bothering to close the door behind him. Sarah muttered to herself

"At least he didn't slam it".

Sarah just sits there for a moment. A colleague, Amy, suddenly comes to the doorway.

"What was that all about"?

"Nothing but a sleep paralysis case with disturbing nightmares. His collective unconscious is exploding like a nuclear bomb" .

"Collective Unconscious. That's mumbo jumbo psychobabble. You just have to go along with what they are saying Sarah. Make them feel listened to".

Sarah is a little flustered. "Well I tried to teach the guy some reality. You know, because, well it's important to be able to distinguish between reality and fiction don't you think".

"Now I see why he stormed off. Don't bring your troubles to work with you Sarah. Especially in this job".

"Ok Amy. Anything you say Amy. Three bags full Amy".

Now it was Amy approaching Sarah although she remained professional unlike the understandably emotional Richard. She calmly says

"If you need to take some time out, cancel the rest of your appointments and take the rest of the day off".

Suddenly Lara appeared at the door.

"That sounds like a great idea Andrea".

"Amy, my name is Amy"

"Amy is right isn't she Sarah"?

Sarah looked directly at Lara and in an exaggerated welcoming tone says "Lara! You must be my next analysand. Have you come here to seek help over your addiction to trying to break up marriages?"

Amy rolled her eyes and walked away.

And then Lara's answer stunned Sarah almost as much as if she was fully aware that she were being abducted by aliens.

"Your marriage is over Sarah. I have spoken to Mike and told him that you are bored with him and that you are just starting to embark on an affair… with me".

Sarah hit the accelerator in her car, breaking the speed limit to get home. Lara had said that she saw Mike at his and Sarah's house, and not at the bookshop. And although she was driving like she was a motorcar racing driver she had no idea what she was going to say to Mike when she arrived. Her head was mangled, her emotions replacing her thoughts. Things were getting too much for her as she used one hand to grip the steering wheel and the other to wipe tears away from her face. And even if she had come up with some well-planned speech she would never have got to say any of it to her husband. Because when Sarah arrived home, Mike was nowhere to be seen. He didn't even leave a note. And Sarah had looked for one. As she did so, another flickering memory surfaced into her consciousness. Or given that it lasted about 3 seconds it could be considered more than a flickering. The memory was of her bedroom. And it was like Richard had described... awash with light and a grey alien staring at her out of its huge almond shaped eyes.

"It can't be" Sarah said to herself. And then she laughed as she started joking about her life to herself. In her mind she was saying, what can't be happening Sarah? That your husband has left you, your best friend wannabe lesbian lover is 100% the cause... or... is it the false memories of alien abduction that cannot be? Sarah's jokey reflection certainly contained inaccuracies. Lara was not the 100% cause of the end of her marriage. Sarah had been falling out of love with Mike and deep down enjoying Lara's attention... so it was partly her own fault. Sarah's nightly experiences were also impacting on her mind and had played their part in the end of her marriage. And Sarah was wrong to think of her abduction experiences as "false memories". They were very real experiences. Literally real experiences.

Lara Hine's ability to be direct and just go for what she wants in relation to Sarah is explained by the fact that they had been best friends for just over 20 years. It gave Lara the confidence or arrogance to be forward at all times. She had no shyness of her friend slash lover. And this over confidence was on display in this very moment as she pulled up in her car outside Sarah and Mikes house.

Lara rang on the doorbell and Sarah, who had seen her coming, answered the door within two seconds.

"I don't f*****g believe it. The nerve of you to show up here".

Lara was taken back. Very rarely had Sarah spoken to her quite like that.

"Hey, we are best friends"

"Oh really, because I thought we were lovers. That is why my marriage is over, right?"

"Oh come on Sarah. You don't love Mike. I have done you a huge favour. But hey, you got the first bit right"

"I am going to do what I thought my patient was going to do this morning"

"And what is that exactly"?

Sarah slams the door hard. Lara, slightly shocked, instinctively tips her head back as it slams shut with a loud thud inches from her face. Lara opens the mailbox and shouts

"Come on Sarah, be reasonable".

"Go away Lara. I never want to see you again".

That stung Lara. A tear fell from her eye and ran down her face. She started to walk away from the house while shouting

"You don't mean that Sarah. I will call you tomorrow".

So the day ended for Sarah with her husband and best friend out of her life. Still she would be receiving some exotic company to compensate before the next morning.

It took much longer for Sarah to go to sleep that night. As a psychiatrist it was obvious to her that anyone who kept thoughts going round and round in their conscious mind would struggle to sleep. It would keep them awake. So she was well aware of why she was still awake as she lay staring at the ceiling at 1 oclock in the morning. She couldn't stop thinking about Mike and Lara. But her day had tired her out so despite the thoughts the lights eventually went out and she eventually attained deep sleep. Almost 2 hours went by seemingly instantly when suddenly she awoke, as shocked as she could possibly feel, with her room lit up like a Christmas tree and a grey alien at the end of her bed beckoning her to come towards it. Sarah reacted by moving back as far as possible. She went to cover her face with her bed covers but she couldn't take her eyes off the thing. And then she levitated in the air. She was again thinking "THIS CAN'T BE HAPPENING"… but this time it was happening multiplied by about a trillion. Suddenly she was aboard a craft. She observed the inside was perfectly circular. She was laid down on a table but was able to look around. There were about 8 or maybe 9 greys present. They all gathered around the table and looked down on her. One of them communicated with Sarah telepathically saying only

"You know we are real".

The next thing Sarah was aware of was her eyes popping open back home in her bed. Then she looked at her bedside clock and it was 11.15am. She was stunned. Impossible she thought. Sarah was convinced she had only been gone for a few minutes and yet the time indicated several hours had gone by. She got up and as normal she went to the bathroom. Only this time rather than admiring herself in the mirror, she instead looked in the mirror and screamed.

Lara genuinely believed in what she had done. She really did think Sarah would be better off with her rather than Mike. She didn't hate Mike but there was clearly a selfish part to her motivation to split them up. But she did think it for the best all round. It was selfish, it was love, it was what she thought was best for all. And she was scheming. She was convinced that either Mike or Sarah, or both, would try and contact one another. Lara thought that scheming like this never works on small screen Netflix drama's or big screen Hollywood movies. But this is real life so she could make it work. The first part of her plan is the most difficult. At least get Sarah to like her again as her best friend. Ahh, she already does care about me thought Lara. She's just pissed off with me. Give her a-little time. Lara then thought that with Sarah back as her best friend, part 2 would be easy to achieve. Sarah really likes me thought Lara so we will be lovers in no time. But that had to happen really fast before Mike and Sarah try and reconcile. Part 3 is the smarty pants bit of the plan. Get Mike to come into the house just at the point where I'm coming out of the shower with Sarah. That will end all Mikes hopes that he had rebuilt, shattering them completely. It's for the best. There's no future for Mike with Sarah.

Lara had an idea in her head for Part 3 of the plan. But the first part was what she was most uncertain about. She went to the Boston Mental Health Institute expecting to find Sarah there. But Amy saw her and told her that Sarah hadn't turned up today. Lara defended Sarah saying she's got problems with her husband. Given the altercation yesterday between Sarah and Lara, Amy suspected that Lara was the cause of that problem although she slanted towards minding her own business.

Lara called at Sarah's. The door was open so Lara just walked in.

"We have to talk" said Lara.

"Foreplay"?

"You are having problems. I am here for you".

"You are the problem Lara". Tears fell from Sarah's eyes. Sarah was down but not lashing out. Lara had feared a barrage of verbal abuse.

"I don't think you really believe that".

"I do believe that".

"Not deep down you don't".

Sarah walked from one room to another, entering the kitchen. She was not saying much and what she was saying was motivated by emotion rather than anything truthful that would stand the test of time. Eventually she composed herself and said

"It's your lucky day Lara".

"Well you can't leave it at that. What do you mean exactly"?

"I can't handle my insanity alone. I think I was…"

"You think you were what?"

"I can't say it but I admit that I need you".

That brought a tear of concern and love to fall from Lara's eye. She moved over to Sarah and hugged her.

"I'm here for you. I always will be".

"I'm going insane Lara".

"But you know that you can tell me anything. You always have done".

"I know better than anyone that you are open minded but this is too much even for you. Look, I had an analysand yesterday. He was having terrifying nightmares, visions, psychological experiences of alien abduction".

"And that's happening to you, right?" said Lara thinking she can read Sarah like a book.

"Well the analysand considered them real experiences"

"And this relates to you, how? You are having horrific nightmares about aliens?"

"Yes but I… I think they… look I do not believe in alien abduction but…".

"Oh my god, you think you really were abducted"?

Sarah puts her elbows on the breakfast bar table and her head between her hands, pauses and eventually says

"Yes".

Lara, usually the more open-minded of the two says

"Sarah. As a psychiatrist you must have doubts about that, surely?"

"Yes. I understand that a person can be asleep and dream of a loud noise in their dream. They can wake up because of it and think it has happened in their home. They can go back to sleep and this can happen over and over again throughout the night. A person can be woke up by their own dream content seven times a night, easily".

"So, there you are then. What appears outer is inner. That explains your abduction".

"But its much more than just a loud bang. It is more real than this. Oh God, now I sound like my analysand. I am practically quoting him".

"I tell you what. It is a little role reversal, but I empathise with you always. I will support you. You know I am open-minded and I know that you are rational, logical, and are no fantasist. So this means I can genuinely wonder if this is really happening to you. You are lucky you know…

"Lucky?" Sarah says with disbelief.

"Yeah. If you were a UFO buff I would be less inclined to believe you. Now I am unsure. And I know abit about UFOs. I have heard of Lue Elizondo and Jacques Vallee and I know about the Roswell incident".

"But you don't buy into abduction until now"?

"Nah, But you experiencing it moves the abduction issue into my open mind".

"I have to admit that if this were you Lara claiming alien abduction, I would be analysing you".

"So we are friends again"?

"Of course. Come here you".

Lara and Sarah hug again. Lara had deliberately kept Mike out of the conversation but couldn't do so any longer.

"What about Mike"?

"Well things haven't been what they were when we first got together. And this is what you want right"?

"I… I… only want what is best for you".

"Well I don't know right now".

"Of course. I will shut up about it. But I should stay the night. You said yourself that you need me".

"Ok, sounds like a plan".

Lara thought that Sarah's choice of words were ironic taking into account that she was unsure how far to go with her plans. She thought to herself that she could tell Mike that Sarah was claiming alien abduction. That would be too much for him right now and would further distance him from her. But that is just wrong. Too much. She couldn't do that to Sarah. She had to be there for her over that issue. Because whatever it is that is happening to her is making her question her sanity. She couldn't use that as a weapon. Indeed, Lara was wondering if she could even go through with the shower idea. This was due to her thinking Mike is a decent guy. He hasn't done anything wrong to Sarah. He just isn't right for her. He doesn't make her feel alive. She deserves better. Yeah. I think I will go through with that plan. But first Sarah needs to see me as more than her best friend.

That night Lara says to Sarah that she should take more days off work. At first Sarah says no but is persuaded by Lara to take a couple of days off. Then Sarah ponders Lara's intentions and says

"You are sleeping in that makeshift bed next to me tonight. Not in the same bed".

"Oh ok".

"You can sleep in one of the spare bedrooms if you want?"

"No. And not because of any desires… but because of your alien problem. Sorry I didn't know how else or how better to put it".

"My psychotic breakdown"?

"You are not psychotic" Lara, knowing the house about as well as she knows her own house, then goes to fetch a bottle of wine.

"Let's just relax and hope for a peaceful night".

But that night was not peaceful. Not for either of them.

Sarah woke up to a strange humming sound, and before she could even open her eyes, she felt herself being lifted off the bed. Her heart racing, she tried to scream, but no sound escaped her lips. She was paralyzed. As she was being carried through the air, Sarah couldn't help but wonder, yet again, if this was really happening. Is it just a super real dream?

The fear of the unknown was overwhelming.

As Sarah was strapped onto a cold metal table, she tried to make sense of what was happening. She looked around the room and saw other people lying on similar tables, their bodies covered in strange instruments and wires. Suddenly, one of the grey aliens approached her, its large black eyes staring into hers. Sarah felt a surge of panic rise within her as she realized that this was not a dream.

Meanwhile, Lara had also been taken by the aliens. She caught a glimpse of Sarah on another table but didn't realize it was her friend until it was too late. As Lara tried to call out to Sarah, one of the aliens silenced her with a sharp look.

Sarah's mind raced as she tried to come up with an explanation for what was happening. Maybe it was all an hallucination. But deep down, Sarah knew that these explanations were just coping mechanisms for her fear.

As the aliens examined her body, Sarah couldn't help but feel violated and helpless. She wanted to fight back, to scream and run away, but her body refused to obey her commands. She was at the mercy of these otherworldly beings, and there was nothing she could do about it. Fortunately the otherworldly beings did nothing that physically hurt her.

Sarah and Lara were returned unharmed, but forever changed by the experience.

"I saw you" said Lara. "I saw you inside the craft"

Sarah sat up in her bed and stared at Lara. The two women embraced one another.

Sarah started to cry, and while embracing Lara asked "Why us Lara? Why us?"

"You know something Sarah. I have always wanted to believe in this stuff"

"For f***s sake Lara. You can't seriously be getting a buzz out of this".

"It was, is, f*****g terrifying. But part of me is getting something out of this, yes."

"What? You mean getting closer to me"?

"No. That's not what I meant" replied Lara momentarily speaking as fast as Grant Cameron. "I mean, answers to questions that have always been of fascination to me. Think about it Sarah, they aren't harming you. You are ok. And they haven't harmed me. I am not an expert but I know enough to know that abductees don't tend to say that the ET's harm them".

"Don't 'TEND' to"?

"They aren't intending to harm us Sarah. That's a good thing".

"Where you going?" asked Sarah as Lara walked out of the room.

"Wine"

"Its 8am. Oh yayy, only about 6 and a half hours of missing time this time".

"Exactly, it still feels like a drinkable time" said Lara who was really looking for Sarah's cell phone so as to text message Mike to come round at a certain time while she's just getting out of the shower with Sarah, both only covered by towels. But she stopped in her tracks. This scheming didn't seem necessary anymore. And the timing would have to be almost perfect. And who knows how it would play out for herself? And the shared abduction changes everything. Lara walked back into the bedroom.

"Err, where's the wine?" asked Sarah.

"You were right. Only alcoholics drink at this time. Save it for later".

"And there was me thinking you had changed your mind about drinking due to travel sickness".

"See that's better. Joking about it already. You could easily have been too traumatized for joking".

"Do you know why I don't have PTSD?"

"Nope."

"Because this time it was a shared alien abduction… with the woman I am in-love with".

Sarah popped into work to tell them of her marital problem and to request a couple of days off which was not only accepted, they offered longer. But Sarah declined their offer for her to take as long as she needs. Back at the house Lara was thinking more about the nature of reality than she was about Sarah. She went online and checked out social media. On twitter she discovered, and was intrigued by Post Disclosure Worlds twitter account as well as Richard Dolan's Intelligent Disclosure twitter account. She checked Dolan out more as she discovered that he accepted abduction as literally real. Just as she was about to purchase one of Dolan's books on Amazon she thought she heard someone try to get into the house. And indeed, in walked Mike, who not surprisingly, given this is his home, had keys to unlock the door.

"Oh F**k" shouted Lara. "Does that guy ever do any work at his own bookshop. F**k, he's gonna go ape-shit".

"Hi Mike" said Lara nervously.

"Where's Sarah. Is she here?" asked Mike angrily.

"No, she's at work. What made you think she would be here?"

"She lives here you home-wrecker".

"No need to be like that. She might live here but she works as a psychiatrist remember".

"Yes but I thought, given that you had destroyed her marriage she might be at home, feeling ill in some way. Instead I find the home-wrecker herself in my home!"

"Mike you are a nice guy. A friend…

"Your not a friend of mine"

"But you are not making Sarah happy."

"Get out! Get out of my home!"

"Err, Sarah wants me here, to look after her. She's feeling unwell. And I'm sorry but she wants to be with me. We slept together last night" said Lara, telling a lie. However the truth would have been much harder to believe.

"You f*****g bitch"

"Think about it Mike. It's morning. I'm here. I was open about wanting Sarah to be more than best friends. I tell you what, if you don't believe me, I will phone her up and tell her that I can't wait to shower with her when she gets back". Lara started to dial the number but Mike fuelled with hatred but certain that she was telling the truth stormed out of his own house. So Lara had not gone through with the shower idea but she had still put it to use in a way. She felt awesome. Total success. Albeit she also felt bizarre, confused and bewildered multiplied by a trillion over what she had experienced last night. Her mild interest in UFOs was more than mild now. Her interest in UFO's had gone through the roof and out of the solar system. And she was in love and sharing this cosmic reality with that person she is in-love with. Tonight will be a great night Lara thought to herself. But will I… indeed will 'we' get abducted again? I f*****g hope not otherwise I will be calling into the Boston Mental Health Institute myself. Oh… and should I tell Sarah that Mike called? Lara answered the Mike question with a firm 'No'.

Lara was taking last night's abduction extremely well relative to most people who have gone through the same ordeal. And Sarah was drawing strength from the fact that she had Lara with her sharing the very same abduction experience. Lara even seemed to be embracing it which shocked Sarah given the potential for such a mind-blowing experience to traumatise experiencers.

That night Lara had candle-lit Sarah's entire house.

"We don't need these candle-lights. We use UFO-lighting, the finest lights on the market" joked Sarah.

She continued "I feel like we are living through one of your short stories. That one where two people fall madly in love while simultaneously being scared shitless due to the fact that they are living in one of the world's most haunted houses."

Lara's face lit up to match the house… and she said "I love that book. It's awesome". Lara was so absorbed in her attempt to get Sarah to fall in-love with her she somehow missed the fact that Sarah had implied it. It was like missing an open goal in a soccer match.

"Wow Lara. You are really egotistical".

"Nah, I'm 12 percent joking. Anyway, enough of the jokes. This should be more intimate an occasion. Take some of this shit. It's supposed to really get to what you might call 'the collective unconscious'. It opens up your mind".

"Geez Lara. I'm supposed to be more Freud than Jung. The only Jung book I have read is The Psychogenesis of Mental Disease. Jung was still kinda Freudian when he penned it".

"Sshhh. You know his theory though. And you are moving on right?"

"If having a more screwed up psyche means becoming more Jungian, then yes, I'm rather fundamentalist right now".

"Hhmmm, that's not an open mind Sarah. You naughty girl" said Lara while moving towards her girlfriend. "So are you going to take the DMT or are you going to take me?"

"Lara. You know me. Wine please. I like to maintain control."

"Control??? You are getting abducted by aliens against your will. Maybe the aliens will be more impressed with a Jungian Shaman than they would be a stuffy Freudian".

Sarah takes hold of the pipe that Lara had dangling infront of her eyes and smokes it. About one second later Sarah is having a coughing fit.

"Ha Ha Ha. You know Sarah, that you get higher if you cough".

"I have messed up my mind. I might as well mess up my lungs".

"You are with me now. Your mind is cured."

"My first girlfriend at 37. I took my time."

"I know you slow coach. I'm only 36 and I'm there already".

Sarah goes sombre as she experiences a moment that Lue Elizondo expects people to experience when the real nature of reality hits them. She says

"How do you do it Lara? How do you stay so amazing following an alien abduction? You don't seem to be experiencing any PTSD symptoms whatsoever".

"In your language there's some Freudian repression and Jungian mask. But its mainly thanks to you. If I had experienced that on my own and if I were lonely I don't think I would cope as well. I also rationalize that the beings return us safely".

"I didn't see the truth" replies Sarah.

"And what is that exactly"?

"That we don't know what the truth is. I mean are we like insects compared to them where intelligence is concerned?"

"Fascinating isn't it?"

"Not really for me. You provide me with comfort, I admit that. But we don't know anything. We see these beings but we don't know what they are like. We just feel subordinate to them".

"It's making you more humble?"

"Yeah, something like that. But more afraid than you are. I don't understand reality anymore. I don't understand the nature of reality."

"It's weird you saying that when you have just experienced 'Super-Reality'"

"I think you embrace it more than I do. It quietens me, humbles me. You get a high out of it."

"hhhmmm, that might just be what I am smoking."

"Lara, there was a sign in the UFO… don't take DMT and ride those babies".

Lara laughs and jokes that she deliberately put off taking DMT until after the abduction. Sarah then makes the point that

"Super Reality is an excellent way of putting it".

"Yeah" says Lara. "We all say its more real than real, not just abductees but Near Death Experiencers as well".

"So this is my new crowd then. DMT, Abductee, Empathy with people who claim to have taken a trip to the afterlife, and cheating with my best friend".

"We aint cheating Sarah. We are meant to be together. Even the extraterrestrials know it. That's why they took us together"

Sarah rolls her eyes and declares "Naturally".

"Hey Sarah. You don't have to dump Freudian Psychoanalysis completely. Your ex will need a Super hot shrink. That shrink cannot be you. Because you are mine. But yeah, another super hot shrink who can do that what's it called? You know Sarah, in the psychoanalytical literature when the patient starts projecting love onto the shrink"?

"Transference"

"Yes, that's it. Transference".

"You are about as ethical as the extraterrestrials Lara".

"Why's that unethical? It sorts out his problem and ensures he leaves us alone. We have enough to deal with, with stalking aliens without having stalker Mike to deal with."

"Don't forget he's still my husband you stalker."

Lara is getting more and more light headed and responds

"I bet your soon to be ex-husband is removing my short stories from his book shop right now. Credit where it's due though, he's a horny mother f****r but you know, I prefer you. Does that turn you on"?

"Maybe. I can see myself with you. Interesting to know you viewed my husband as a horny mother f****r. But good news. I was lying about the maybe I can see myself with you bit".

Sarah continues what she is saying in a deliberately dramatic style. She speaks VERY slowly and walks VERY slowly towards Lara and continues

"I can definitely say that I will soon be removing my husband from my life". As she says this she places her hands on each side of Lara's face and gently kisses her on the lips.

Sarah and Lara sleep together. Sarah moving down Lara's naked body kissing every inch of it. Lara wanting and needing this. Their passion for one another made all the stronger by their astonishing shared experience.

Sarah's psychiatrist colleagues welcome her back with loving support. Joe Preston, who has always had a thing for Sarah, hugged her as she came in. But he had some news for her and he wanted to be the one who gave it to her.

"In the couple of days you have been off work we have suddenly become inundated with patients suffering trauma symptoms. All of those patients claim that what triggered their trauma were either alien abduction nightmares or literal alien abductions. I would of dismissed the literal interpretation but have you seen the breaking news?"

Meanwhile back at Sarah's house, Lara is online checking out the UFO community. She logs onto twitter and runs a search for 'UFO Disclosure'. She then recalls that the other day she had checked out Post Disclosure world and Richard Dolan's UFO pages. She sees a tweet by Post Disclosure World declaring in CAPS LOCK 'THE

HOUSE OF CARDS IS FALLING BABY!!!!!!!!!!!'

There's a link there to a video. She clicks on it. She sees Ryan talking and looking like Jesus Christ. He says "I want to correct myself. I said the House of Cards is falling baby. What I meant to say is that the House of Cards HAS fallen baby". He says this with a huge grin on his face with a glass of champagne in each of his hands while simultaneously a bucket load of confetti is falling onto and around his head. He then gets takes a serious tone (while still drinking his champagne) saying that despite his joy, it is difficult for some people to come to terms with being abducted whereas others are seemingly quickly able to get used to it. It is of primary importance that those people finding this experience traumatic are reassured that no harm will come to them and that this is a positive and necessary part of our evolution as a species. He then finishes his video by playing the Post-Disclosure flute.

Lara reflected on the fact that she and Sarah had come out in two ways recently. As Bi-Sexual and as Abductees. She switched on the TV news because she wanted to consume as much of this miracle as possible. She continued to simultaneously check out the UFO community on twitter. She checked out BBC. There was a reporter in Manchester City Center talking to people just outside a Shopping Mall. People were coming up to the reporter and telling him that they had been abducted and that the UFO Phenomenon is very real. And the reporter was not questioning that fact because he himself had been abducted. There was much talk about the Greys, some fear and reassurance from other shoppers, saying that they are not here to harm us. But then a guy interrupted them all pushing in to get himself positioned right infront of the TV Camera and said "You think the State will welcome this? They are toast! They've been seen through as liars! It's over for those bastards!" The people around him cheered. Lara pondered this: If this is reflected across the world then what will that mean? Then another guy butted in and shouted that the ETs "SIMULATE" our so-called reality. He shouts "What they show us in those abductions is what they want us to see". Lara went back to twitter and looked at the results of another twitter search for 'UFO Disclosure'. Very near to the top of the search results was 'Richard Dolan Intelligent

Disclosure'. He was getting new followers like an A-lister which Lara thought he was becoming as she witnessed the following numbers go up and up and up. He was getting a lot of credit for having been right all along. His view that the State is a Secret State (as opposed to being a democracy) was vindicated. Lara was already vaguely aware of Richard Dolan and would have bought one of his books the other day if Mike hadn't entered the house.

"He should change his first name from Richard to Rich" she said while viewing his page. "Rich Dolan… he should check out his bank balance. I would. Because those books gonna be selling like hotcakes". She clicks on a video that Dolan posted a few hours ago. He is discussing the end of the Secret State. Lara thinks the guy from Manchester she saw on the TV would agree with Dolan. However, Dolan is much more polite (in tone) compared to the guy on TV.

Lara continues flicking through the News Channels on TV. Now she's watching CNN. An Australian UFO Reporter called Ross Coulthart is being interviewed. She missed the start of the interview so doesn't know if it's been celebratory or bringing up some of the more worrying challenges for the coming days. She hears Coulthart say the following…

"The News Media are lapping this Disclosure up like a cat lapping up cream. But when the dust settles the news media is not going to come out of this smelling like a bed of roses." The news woman interviewing him interrupts by asking "Why not? The likes of Leslie Kean, Christopher Sharp and yourself have done outstanding investigative journalism regarding this issue. People owe you a debt of gratitude and you are news media" Coulthart responds by saying "Oh please, come on. You probably hadn't heard of us until about last night. And the public won't be impressed by a few good apples in a field of thousands of bad apples. The UFO community have been aware of nuclear incursions for decades whereas the news media made a choice not to investigate these things. Most of the Post World War 2 news media attitude towards UFO's has been one of ridicule rather than investigative journalism.

Witnesses have been illegally intimidated, threatened, diagnosed as mentally ill and had their careers destroyed. And where was the news media for those people? Nowhere to be seen. So don't be surprised when a barrage of criticism is aimed at the news media from the now dominant UFO community. The news media's inaction deserves about as much criticism as the secret keepers themselves."

Back on twitter she sees a recent albeit PRE-Disclosure tweet from London Journalist, Christopher Sharp (Dated 4 May 2023). He tweeted – "Economic turmoil - Cost of living crisis - War in Ukraine - China & Taiwan - Disruptive AI technology Then there are highly credible sources telling me that the U.S. has recovered craft belonging to non human intelligence. And it's coming out. It doesn't feel real sometimes"

A few days ago Lara would have been moderately curious about such a tweet. Now she thinks EVERYONE believes in recovered craft originating from non-human intelligence!

Although I bet no-one (Christopher Sharp included) thought Disclosure would happen like this! I think I will phone SETI and tell them I have received more than a f*****g signal.

She flicks onto another News Channel. It's all 24/7 Abduction and Disclosure (with some pointing out what will come next). She notices that the channels that are normally a mix of pop culture, documentaries, news, are now just 100% news about the UFO issue. What the news is making Lara think is that no one in authority has declared a UFO Disclosure. Rather it's a spontaneous non-State Disclosure that has happened over night. And with modern communication systems (namely the internet) it has spread like wildfire. Back online Richard Dolan spells it out... "It's an ET-initiated Disclosure". Lara likes how he put it. She thinks and mutters to herself "Yeah, that sounds right".

Lara keeps checking UFO twitter. Grant Cameron is talking so fast in a newly posted video that she can barely understand him. Luckily he plays old videos of him talking to abductees. She observes a subtle difference from what she has heard other abductees say. They talk more about consciousness. She listens a little more and hears about the mind or thought being used to control the UFO craft. Of course she is an abductee herself, but she never experienced that and Sarah hasn't mentioned it either. But Lara thinks it sounds like such an abduction would be much healthier than the more typical abductions you hear about. She wishes Sarah had experienced an abduction where she was given the opportunity to control the craft using the mind rather than being stared at and examined on a table.

She further hears abductees talking about consciousness distorting reality. Lara's vague knowledge of the UFO field makes a connection. She knows that Vallee didn't sign up 100% to the ET hypothesis and thinks that he supports this reality distortion view. But there is so much bombardment from the media about abductions and Disclosure that Lara, experiencing much of Grants excitement herself, cannot resist but try and consume all of it at once. The more she consumes the more her perspective progresses away from recent days being about Sarah and herself. That is important to her still. However, she can see that hundreds of millions of people have been experiencing contact with other-worldly beings. The sheer magnitude of it all suddenly hits home. And she shouts out as loudly as she possibly can "F**K ME!!!! THIS IS A NEW WORLD!!!"

And then she suddenly feels pure love for all of humanity and bursts into tears, feeling astonished with what she is living through.

Lara decides to go and see Sarah at work. When she gets there she is pleased to hear that her girlfriends final patient of the day has rang in to cancel. The person who told her this said the patient feels more at one with the world because he's an abductee. So whereas just a couple of days ago being an abductee made the patient feel the need to seek help from a psychiatrist, now the same patient feels at one with the world and does not feel the need for any mental health help. What a turnaround!

Lara waits for about 20 minutes for Sarah to finish work. She comes out and Lara excitedly starts talking like she's possessed by Grant Cameron. She goes on about the amazing news that people worldwide have been going through "what we have gone through". Lara just wants Sarah to consume some of the news she has consumed. Or to put it more precisely, she wants her girlfriend to experience A LOT of the news she has consumed. So they get in the car and head home.

"We have been through so much but we were never alone. We didn't realize how many others were experiencing this" says Lara.

"Yeah. I could only think of one" replies Sarah thinking of Richard.

"But of course there's always been many abductees who we don't know personally. People didn't believe them but that was only because they hadn't experienced an abduction themselves. This Disclosure has been so quick though. Clearly the intelligence behind these UFOs has disclosed this. Jesus. How long have they been here? How long have they been watching humans? Some abductees claim to have experienced abduction for their entire lives or at least for as long as they can remember. No more psychoanalyzing abduction away as mere sleep paralysis for you Sarah."

"I have learned my lesson on that one."

Sarah is driving and she's one minute away from home. She drives safely around the corner to the street where her house is located. And then she and Lara are gobsmacked.

Rather than seeing the usual row of houses on the street they instead see a beach. Lara looks at Sarah and says

"They play with reality like a toy".

Chapter 2: From Abduction to Disclosure

Push-back. But not from the pre-Disclosure debunkers. The UFO community were now the sceptics where the biological extraterrestrial hypothesis was concerned. At least many of them were. And that was one hell of an irony that was not lost on Sarah Aston and Lara Hine. The New World was often on Lara Hine's mind. And quite often on her girlfriend, Sarah Aston's mind. But right now Lara was simply looking for her lost diary. She cannot find it anywhere. She hunts high and low for it and then, after about 10 minutes an horrendous thought pops into Lara's head. Sarah's husband, Mike had been round the other day collecting the rest of his things. Mike and Sarah were no longer together. Lara had seen to that.

On the outside Lara does not show what she is thinking on the inside. But she is thinking "FUUCCCKKKKKK". Lara thinks that Mike is hoping that her diary will show some wrongdoing. She did consider and write about scheming to win Sarah's love. She had very strongly considered setting Mike up to call round as she and Sarah showered. Had she achieved this the thinking was that Mike would have had his hopes and dreams of winning Sarah back completely shattered. Lara was plotting that goal at a time when she was not with Sarah other than as best friends and Sarah and Mike were husband and wife. They still are but not for much longer unless Lara has made a last minute blunder.

The diary will show that she was even going to use Sarah's cell phone and text him to come to the house at a specific time, i.e., just as Lara would be leaving the shower to oh-so-conveniently see to who it was at the door with a towel wrapped around her with Sarah also in close proximity.

Sarah and Mike, officially speaking, still were husband and wife as their divorce has not gone through. But to all intents and purposes Sarah and Lara were now together as a couple. Lara thinks that Sarah will probably let her off for that scheming plan but there is worse. She also wrote in the diary of another idea which was to use Sarah's alien abductions against her to make Mike think his wife was going insane. In Lara's defense she fairly quickly rejected that plan for the right reason. That reason being that she considered it immoral and crosses a line. She couldn't make Sarah look crazy in the eyes of another person. But will Sarah be angry at her for even considering it? Because Lara is now convinced that Mike has stolen the diary.

Lara does not know what to do about the diary situation. So for now at least she brings up the topic of the UFO Phenomenon which is 24/7 dominating news headlines worldwide.

"I think that Pre Disclosure the believers were far more accurate in their thinking than the debunkers. Maybe sceptics who thought something was going on were always the most accurate. But now that Disclosure has happened I think the sceptics who think something is going on are definitely the adults in the room."

"Well thank you Lara" Sarah says over enthusiastically. "But" Sarah continues, "Now everyone just thinks the believers were 100% right. So what is clear to you is not so much to others".

Lara stares at Sarah, thinking she can work her out like a crossword. "You are still a sceptic of sorts aren't you?"

"Yes. But within a new paradigm or within the context of Post Disclosure".

"So what is it you are sceptical about then?"

"That this new world was the result of extraterrestrials abducting people"

"Yeah, that's what I was meaning. Sceptics are now the sensible ones. There's people who believed in UFO reality for years who are now more sceptical than the man and woman in the street about this being about extraterrestials. But WE were abducted by extraterrestrials weren't we???" Lara asked momentarily experiencing a little cognitive dissonance.

"Surface appearances"

"Huh?"

"Well, we also experienced something that many people have not experienced and that was our street turning into a beach!!! I can't trust surface appearance so-called reality anymore".

"I see what you are saying. You think that a clique of powerful humans might be simulating alien abduction experiences?"

"Too right I do, yes".

Lara then went online and showed Sarah a tweet she found on one of her frequent UFO twitter searches. They were two pre-Disclosure tweets by the American cultural commentator, Eric Weinstein. In one of them he said that "we may be faking a UFO situation? Or that we may be covering up the duplicity of our own "Operation Fortitude" type program?" And he followed that tweet up by saying that it involves classified R & D, spying and deception. In that same tweet he said "something big is going on" but that he is not invested in "little green men".

Sarah asked "Does he still say that it's nothing to do with aliens now that we are past the old world?"

Lara simply answered "Yup".

"Ok, he might be onto something here".

Lara explains… "Yeah, he thinks it's an attempt to create a New dominant myth on Planet earth. The UFO/ET Phenomenon as a cover for the U.S.' most advanced and exotic aerospace R&D".

"Geez, if true then this human clique take it really far with abduction simulations".

"Indeed. But it's worked hasn't it. And that is all the State Superstructure cares about".

Sarah smiles and says "State Superstructure… I never thought I would hear you sound off like some kind of Marxist academic".

Sarah then gets off the UFO topic and approaches Lara in her familiar dramatic slow walk towards her and says… "We are not straight girls anymore. When are we going to have fun again?"

Lara responds "There are no straight girls. There's only girls that haven't met me".

Sarah laughed and said "Is this an ego contest? If it is then just remember the only thing that makes you interesting is me".

"Oh and why would that be?"

"Because I have seen your diary and on the 28th April you wrote "I am nothing without Sarah".

Lara is stunned and doesn't know what to say. She composes herself for a moment and then goes to speak… but just before she does Sarah reassures her…

"Relax, I didn't sit down and treat it like a page turner of a book".

"Err, well why did you read it at all? You know we tell each other everything".

"Shouldn't bother you that I read that flattering comment of yours then should it"?

"Ok Ok OK. So what happened? Did the diary just float across the room, settle down on your lap as you drank a cup of coffee and then magically open up on that page"?

"Mike was here. And…

"Oh I might have guessed. He's trying to find dirt on me, right?"

"Yes, he was. But I snatched the diary off him."

"But you still read some?"

"No. He was reading that out-loud. His eyes were focused on the page he was reading so it was easy to snatch the diary off him. He wasn't going to physically assault me to get it back. You do seem a bit uptight about this Lara. Is there something in that diary you don't want me to see?"

Lara was kicking herself for not staying more cool under pressure. Sarah now suspected something was going on. Lara tells Sarah to give her the diary so she can show her something she doesn't really want her to see. Sarah goes to collect the diary from another room. Lara is feeling tense. Sarah gives her it. Lara then shows her the entries about planning the shower scene and also the short-lived plan to make Sarah look crazy by telling Mike she thinks she's being abducted by aliens. Of course that was back in the Pre-Disclosure world when such a plan could very well work perfectly. Lara fears the worst. But Sarah responds

"Thank you Lara. You have done the right thing".

"I haven't missed anything out. There isn't anymore".

"I didn't think there was".

"How would you know?"

"Because I lied. I didn't snatch the Diary out of Mikes hands. I did however, tell him to give the diary to me. But he read out the very extracts that you have quoted to me. If there was more scheming plans he would have read those out to me as well".

"And you are ok with that?" said Lara, thinking she might have got away with it, but still worried that she might not have done.

"Yes because you didn't go through with the plot to make me look crazy. We have also been through so much since then. And also because you were honest right now. I might have had a problem with you if you hadn't fessed up just now. Also, Mike is desperate and is turning rather sociopathic. I think he needs to get mental health help. I wouldn't go back to Mike in any conceivable scenario. I think he is going literally crazy. Obviously I can't say that to him though with me being his wife who left him for my best friend, and with me being a psychiatrist. It would sound like I was offering my psychiatric services".

Sarah continues… "You said something special in that diary. You said that you are nothing without me. I saw that when Mike finally handed the diary over. You said it in the same entry as the shower plan".

Lara does an impression of Sarah slowly dramatically walking up to her. She opens the diary randomly on multiple pages. Whatever page she opens up there is a statement from Lara saying that she is nothing without Sarah.

Sarah smiled. And said "I think about you all the time Lara. I think about your eyes and your mouth, your hair, what clothes you might wear, your secret thoughts, what you might be dreaming about as I lay beside you, I just wanna know everything about you".

Lara listened. When Sarah finished speaking there was a pause and Lara said "I think about you too. I mean I masturbate about you a lot".

Sarah didn't know whether Lara was joking or not. Taken aback she responded by deflecting.

"I wonder what the latest UFO news is"? as she switched on the television. True, Sarah put the TV on so as to deflect from the awkwardness. However what she and Lara saw was a riot in New York City. The cause? Multiple high level State Officials whistle-blowing. What those whistle blowers were saying was that some within the State had known about UFO's for 75 years but covered it up because they did not know the origins of the intelligence behind the craft. The whistle-blowers also said some sections of the State were well aware of the abductions.

Leslie Kean, now working as a reporter for CNN is on the streets of New York City as petrol bombs are being thrown at the police, shop windows smashed, cars set on fire. Nevertheless Leslie remains professional, microphone in hand, speaking above the noise all around her to update people on what is going on. She was given the unenviable task of reporting from NYC's riot-laden streets because she is one of the few reporters that people still trust given that she was one of the few reporters who had spent years trying to get people to respect the UFO issue. This meant that the people saw her as on their side and fighting their battles. While people saw most Big News Media as complicit in a cover-up as they rarely applied investigative journalism to the Phenomenon throughout the post World War 2 period.

Leslie Kean reporting from New York City… "For many people their abduction experience was their Disclosure. But it was the admission from those within classified clandestine programs that elements within the State have known about the abductions for 75 years that has brought about scenes like the ones you can see here all around me. These riots are occurring in many major cities around the world. The confessions that have been made by State insiders are viewed by many as a Second Disclosure. The first being their own abduction experiences that hundreds of millions of people experienced, perhaps but not necessarily that first Disclosure being ET-initiated and now this Disclosure that a tiny minority of officials within the State, including President Eisenhower and John F Kennedy, were briefed on the abductions. Knowledge of such a cover-up has triggered these scenes and my word, what a cover-up it was. It was more top-secret than the

Atomic Bomb. It is a miracle that the secret ever got out. So if you are just tuning in, I will repeat, because this is a momentous moment in human history… It was the Whistle-blowers from A Special Activities Division of the State, a Clandestine or Covert Intelligence Agency have just in the last hour and a half admitted that elements within the State has been aware of abductions of humans taking place for 75 years and that two Presidents over that time were briefed on this. They also confess to knowing about the Phenomenon more widely such as the ability to transform the reality of the experiencers immediate environment perhaps in a similar or same way as the simulated abductions if that is what they are. The origins issue concerning what this is… is still causing a conflict of it's own. There is still so much uncertainty surrounding the origins of the intelligence behind all of this such as what is the intelligence behind the abductions. Many questions remain unanswered such as was the Roswell crash an alien craft? It's like the factions war within the State concerning what the intelligence is has now been given to the rest of us, to the UFO community and now to the people as a whole. Indeed, it strikes me that everyone now sees themselves as part of the UFO community. This is truly the People's issue on a grand scale. The State secrecy was for more than one reason. But the whistle-blowers say the key was so that the State maintains power and control over the people. It was considered as impossible for governments to confess that they were not in control of their own airspace and seas… and considered impossible to admit that they were powerless to protect people from abduction. People had already suspected that the State was well aware of what was going on when what was originally considered the spontaneous ET-led Disclosure happened last month. However, no one knows whether they can trust what the State is saying any more. Maybe they carried out the abductions in some simulated sense. Maybe they are working with some other-worldly intelligence".

Suddenly a highly aggravated and distraught man snatches the microphone out of the reporters hand and despite crying as he spoke, he was still intelligible as he could be heard shouting into the camera "My brother committed suicide over his abduction. How many others went through the same thing? I don't want to live in a world like this anymore". He slams the microphone to the ground and then walks onto the road just as a Yellow Cab comes speeding towards him. It hits him at high speed and kills him almost instantly.

"Oh my God" shouts Sarah watching this happen live on her TV.

"Ouch" says Lara.

Sarah instantly turns her head towards Lara… gobsmacked and open-mouthed at Lara's lack of real empathy.

"Ouch. Is that your response to that? Really"?

"Who the hell knows what is going on anymore? How do I know this isn't a Simulation, maybe that was or wasn't a simulation. I don't understand reality anymore. The simulators can convince us that we are being abducted by aliens, they can convince us our street is a beach. Maybe they simulate all of those Near Death Experiences too. Maybe that guy is experiencing a blissfully simulated Near Death Experience. Maybe there's hundreds or thousands of Simulated Matrix worlds. So yeah, Ouch is my response".

"Thanks for that Lara. Now I think reality is one big hallucinatory Schizophrenia".

"It is. And you are a psychiatrist. So enjoy your new found wealth".

The riots were spreading across the U.S. LA was rioting, Chicago was rioting, San Franscisco was rioting. And so were the major cities of Europe. Berlin was rioting, London was rioting, Milan was rioting, and Paris was of course rioting. It should be no surprise then that Sarah and Lara decided to go to Sarah and Mikes Lake-side house.

They were both convinced that it was only a matter of time (probably hours or merely minutes) before Boston became a city of large scale rioting. They get in the car and as they do so they both fail to notice a stealthy Mike sat in a car nearby spying on them. As the two women drive off, Mike follows them.

It didn't require hours or even minutes for Boston to join in the rioting. It had already started before the couple had even left their Boston home. As they drive, Sarah and Lara encounter a chaotic scene of rioting and destruction. Buildings are on fire, windows are smashed, and people are running in every direction. The sounds of sirens and shouting fill the air, creating a sense of danger and urgency.

As they drive further away from the city, the chaos begins to fade away. They pass by small towns and villages, where people are going about their daily lives. Farmers tend to their crops, children play in the streets, and families sit on their porches enjoying the warm summer evening.

As they approach the lake-side home, the scenery becomes more serene and peaceful. The roads wind through dense forests and rolling hills, with occasional glimpses of the shimmering lake in the distance.

As Sarah and Lara arrive at the peaceful lakeside house, it's hard for them to believe that civilization is seemingly collapsing just a short drive away from where they are. They are immediately struck by the breath-taking view. The house was perched on a small hill overlooking the lake, with large windows that allowed for an unobstructed view of the water. The lake was calm and still, reflecting the beautiful colours of the sky above. The sun was just beginning to set, casting a warm golden glow over everything.

The house itself was a charming wooden structure, with a large porch that wrapped around the front and side. The porch was furnished with comfortable chairs and a small table, perfect for enjoying a morning cup of coffee or an evening glass of wine while taking in the view.

Inside, the house was cosy and inviting. The living room had plush sofas arranged around a fireplace, with large windows that provided even more views of the lake. The kitchen was fully equipped with modern appliances and plenty of counter space for cooking and entertaining.

The bedrooms were located on the second floor, each with its own balcony overlooking the lake. The beds were dressed in soft linens and fluffy pillows, promising a comfortable night's sleep after a day spent exploring the nearby town or simply relaxing by the water.

"This is the real reason why I stole you from your husband. To get you here then kill you and keep the Lake-side house all for myself" jokes Lara.

Sarah laughs and says "I thought you were at least going to credit me with the line… I stole you from Mike so as to be saved from the collapse of civilization… which incidentally, I am doing. This is stunning".

Lara breathes in the air, admires the beauty of the lake and then says "I do feel rather lucky right now".

"Me too. There is a problem though".

"What's that?"

"We can't stay here long. I can't pull an endless sickie. People at the Mental Health Facility already probably suspect me of doing so. If I am wrong about that and they think I am down with the flu again then it won't be long before some of them would start to suspect".

"Grrrr. Don't spoil it Sarah. Let's just stay here forever".

Lara heads for the Lake House.

Sarah observes her girlfriend heading for the door and she stops her in her tracks by saying … "Have you forgot something?" Sarah waves the door keys in the air.

"I never thought you would need keys around here. It's so secluded and remote".

"Well it's locked so here you go. Now you can go in". Sarah throws Lara the keys and she manages to make the catch.

"Oh how rustic" says Lara as she approaches the door…
"Not really your or my style and yet somehow I like it".

Lara enters the house with Sarah following behind her.

"Hhhmmm, criticism and praise. Very confusing. It's not rustic inside though. You see a bit of wood and you think something is rustic."

"Well I'm a city girl so excuse my ignorance. Anyway it's beautiful. I had almost forgotten how beautiful and peaceful this place is. I thirst for this now".

Having explored the inside of the house Lara is back to one of her other passions… the UFO community, especially UFO Twitter.

Now let's get a bit more modern" says Lara going online.

"Time to check out what the simulators are up to".

"Haven't we come here to get away from all of that"? asks Sarah while dreaming of doing something more intimate with Lara.

"Well… for me it's about getting away from the riots and all the terrifying destruction".

"There's an inextricable link between the simulators and the destruction."

"They might NOT be simulators of course. That's your theory and I like it. But many others disagree".

"Such as who"?

"That's what I am going online to check. Give me a sec".

Lara is back on UFO Twitter. She tells Sarah that Garry Nolan, an American immunologist, academic, inventor, business executive, and UFO researcher leans heavily towards a paranormal answer to the phenomenon. Meanwhile Silicon Valley figures such as Sam Altman are pushing the Simulation theory as the answer to the origins of the intelligence behind the abductions. So it is the techies that Sarah is supporting. Most of those Silicon Valley figures opt for the State doing clandestine black ops Simulations rather than extraterrestrial initiated abductions. The cultural commentator Eric Weinstein has a similar view. Meanwhile both Sarah and Lara are a little intrigued by Michael Masters, a Professor of biological anthropology, who is pushing the human time-traveler theory. Finally, Lara says "The General Public still seem to think its extraterrestrial but some public figures think that will lessen over time. The extraterrestrial hypothesis is certainly being challenged a lot and yet remember when all of this first came out… it seemed like everyone now knew what this was all about. It was all about ET initiated Disclosure"

"Right now I don't care Lara. I'm just glad to be away from it all".

Sarah may have been away from being surrounded by the city of Boston's violence. But her ex husband was having violent thoughts against her, and especially against Lara who he blamed for the collapse of his marriage. And he was lurking merely yards away from the Lake-side House.

Mike Aston was a defeated man. Civilization collapsing around him, his marriage collapsed already, his mental health in tatters, his income falling like a stone. You see, his material comfort derived mostly from his wife's income as a psychiatrist whereas his book store was a distant second in terms of earnings. Lara had humiliated him. His hatred for her growing to a point of being out of control. Lara was a short story writer and he had always given pride of place to her books in his store. Not anymore. He removed them from the store and set fire to every single one of them. He had thought he could win Sarah back but Lara was one step or ten steps ahead every-time. Or maybe she was just right and Sarah simply preferred her. Now Mike was in the mind-state that looters are in when a bomb drops on a city during a war. Just do whatever the hell you want. Nobody cares anymore and law and order is finished. He considered his life and humanity's life as over. And he wanted to take Sarah and Lara down with him. This attitude of not giving a shit anymore felt 100% true to Mike until he got within yards of the Lake-House. Then he started to bottle it. I can't go through with it he thought to himself. He was unprepared to just attack Sarah or Lara or even to merely start threating to do so. This irked and irritated the living hell out of Mike. He simultaneously hated them but felt unable to do anything about it. This was a conflicted mind that his wife would surely be able to explain. Maybe her new Jungian attitude would say that the shadow wanted to become a full monster but there was still some of the old formerly dominant morality holding it back in a battle for supremacy. His inner conflict certainly felt painful to him.

Mike got back in his car. Kept it hidden from view and indecisively considered his options.

He sat there for several hours pondering those options unable to decide what to do. Yes, his mental illness had got that bad. Eventually he saw Sarah and Lara walk out the house. The two women were simply going for a pleasant leisurely walk out. This brought about some level of decisiveness in Mikes mind. He decided to walk into the house and then when Sarah and Lara returned they would be shocked to find him there. He would then ensure they felt worse than shock. He would make them pay for what they have done to him. Luckily for Mike the women had left the door unlocked as Mike did not have a key.

It was a 45 minute wait for Sarah and Lara to return. But when he finally sees his wife and former friend returning he again bottles it and hides under the bed. Mike is turning out to be as spineless as he is angry.

Then Sarah and Lara enter the bedroom. They are literally in the same room as him. And they are in a rather joyful mood despite not having downed any alcohol yet. "Sarah smiles at Lara. 'You know I've always admired you,' she said.

Lara's cheeks turned pink. 'What do you mean?'

'You're just...so beautiful, and kind, and confident. I've always wanted to be like you' and then in exaggerated style planted a kiss on Lara's forehead.

Mike watched from his hiding place, seething. How could Sarah be falling for this manipulative woman? He had to intervene, to remind Sarah of the life they had built together.

But he couldn't. A mental block prevented him from intervening. He heard Lara's response to Sarah: 'You should never try to be somebody else, Sarah. Especially not for me.'

Mike hesitated, listening as the conversation shifted from admiration to flirtation. He felt a cold, hard knot of anger in his chest. How dare they? How dare they betray him like this?

But he couldn't storm out and confront them. Not yet. He had to bide his time, to plot his revenge.

Mike thought he had hit rock bottom. But now he really did hit rock bottom as his wife and Lara, sat on the bed and start massaging each other just an arm's length away from him. "How does that feel"? Lara asks Sarah. "F*****g awful" Mike thought to himself. "Blissful" replies Sarah. Then Lara starts kissing Sarah's neck. "And this?" "Even better". Mike wants Sarah to tell Lara that she's a selfish bitch but he knows he has lost that game. Then Sarah and Lara start passionately kissing. Mike thinks his head is going to explode such is its anguish. Mike texts Sarah in a desperate attempt to disturb the intolerable love making that was starting to break out right above him. It works. Sarah checks the message.

"It's Mike".

"What the hell does he want"?

"He's asked me if I hate him or not"?

"What are you replying"?

"No I don't hate you".

"He sounds down and out sending you a text like that"

"He's responded… he's said ok, I will climb down from this ledge".

"Humor can't get around the fact that was a desperate text"

"You are right. I am sending one more text telling him to sort his head out".

Sarah texted Mike and then threw her phone on the floor. Things got worse for Mike who then had to endure hearing his wife groan with pleasure. The women's fingers and hands searched and explored each others bodies, their kissing and their breathing becoming more audible, their movements becoming faster and more intolerable for poor Mike.

Mike had never felt more messed up in his life. His mind was a mess but still just about rational enough for part of it to understand the stupidity of the position he had placed himself in. And that conflict in his mind had been about whether to put the fear of God into Sarah and Lara face to face or not. He had made a decision at last. He did not want to go that far in a face-to-face confrontation. Mike was like many potential murderers who cannot put the literal knife into someone but can literally shoot them from a distance. Thus he could hardly claim to be any more moral than those that would attack face-to-face. Because he was now planning on ramming their car off the road, with his ex wife and his ex friend hopefully seriously injured or killed.

Some people would find Mike's predicament hilarious in terms of having to hear his wife and former friends love making from such close proximity while they were oblivious that he was even there. For Mike it was no laughing matter. It was the straw that broke the camel's back and turned him into a potential murderer. Of course it was lucky for Mike, and for Sarah and Lara, that they hadn't spotted him or heard him. Mike had expertly held back coughs, sneezes and even wind while under that bed.

Mike couldn't breathe much of a sigh of relief after his former loved one's finished making love. He had to endure more talk that he experienced as mental agony piled on top of mental agony.

His wife said "That was amazing. I've never felt so connected to anyone before."

"I've wanted this for so long, Sarah… here with you in this Lake House making love, drinking wine here, enjoying the view and the peace together. You mean everything to me."

"I can't believe we waited so long to get together, Lara."

"I was scared, Sarah. I didn't want to ruin our friendship, but being with you is worth any risk."

"I just want to stay in your arms forever."

"Me too, Sarah. I promise to always be here for you."

Thankfully Sarah and Lara didn't just stay in bed for the rest of the night. If they had done so Mike would have had to stay exactly where he was. But Lara went to fetch a bottle of wine then popped her head back around the door to say "Ahh, I don't know where it is". So Sarah came out while Lara made a snack for herself. At that point Mike made a sharp exit through a window and over the balcony. It was a long way down, but he climbed down relatively successfully but did have to jump from a height that could have caused him an injury. Both Sarah and Lara heard something that seemed to derive from the bedroom. Sarah was the first to speak up. But they approached the bedroom so slowly and cautiously, with Sarah holding a sharp and deadly looking kitchen knife in her hand, that Mike, if he had a ladder could have probably climbed back to the bedroom and escaped again 3 times over.

"Oh shit, we aren't getting abducted again are we"? asked Lara.

"Nah. It's dark in here. Getting abducted is like entering the light in the NDE… frigging blinding".

Then Lara joked "Maybe it was Mike stalking you"

"We can rule that one out as well, he wouldn't have needed to have sent me a text. He could have just asked me face-to-face whether I hated him or not"?

And of course Sarah was right and wrong. Right that he could have asked her the question to her face. But also wrong because he was too weak to dare to disturb her while she was making love to Lara from arms length away.

Mike had slept in his car overnight. He had guessed that Sarah would need to go back to Boston for work. He wasn't sure that he was right but he was experiencing a total mental breakdown so was desperate enough to gamble on it. And sure enough he saw his two enemies placing some belongings in Sarah's car ready to head back home.

Minutes later Sarah and Lara are driving along a secluded road. They are chatting about how much they just want to live in that Lake-Side House, away from all the chaos of civilization.

"I wouldn't have agreed with that two years ago. Back then I was happy with Mike and so comfortable with my psychiatry career" said Sarah. "But now with civilization in meltdown and potential revolutions all over the place, I now couldn't agree more".

Lara didn't respond to that statement. She agreed with it but she had become more interested in the nutcase accelerating fast, from behind them, towards their car.

"I think we might have a lunatic behind us" said Lara.

Sarah glanced at the car mirror and said "I think you might be right". A few seconds later she said "Oh my God".

"What?" asked a worried Lara.

"I know that car. It's Mike's".

"Your shitting me" hit back Lara just as Mike's car hit the back of Sarah's car.

"SPEED UP! SPEED UP!" demanded Lara.

"I'm going as fast as I can"

Total fear was all the two women were feeling right now. Total madness was all the single man was feeling right now.

"Jesus. He's a psychopath" Shouted Lara in a very frightened tone of voice.

Mike speeded up sufficiently to position his car to the side of Sarah's and then he tried to ram Sarah and Lara off the road. Lara screamed.

The women's car skidded dangerously to the side of the road but Sarah managed to maintain sufficient control.

"FASTER! FASTER! FASTER!" screamed Lara.

Sarah managed to get a little ahead of Mike's car. Both Sarah and Mike were driving dangerously fast. Too fast.

Mike shouted out-loud "DIE BITCHES! DIE!" He had a look of extreme determination on his face. Boring Mike had gone completely insane. He put his foot down on the accelerator and was within inches of Sarah's car when suddenly Sarah's car disappeared into thin air.

"WHAT THE F**K!!!!!!" shouted Mike, not able to comprehend in the slightest what just happened right in-front of him. Maybe if he had lived for another minute he might have thought it something to do with the New World everyone was living in. But his next thought was expressed as a scream as he was driving 75 mph and unable to make the necessary turn around the bend. He tried desperately to make the car turn, turning the steering wheel in the direction he wanted the car to go while simultaneously slamming his foot down on the brakes. But it was too late. The car went on two wheels and skidded off the road and went tumbling down a cliff, bursting into flames at the bottom killing Mike instantly on impact with the ground.

"Lara" said Sarah extremely slowly.

"I… what?" Lara shakes her head

Sarah speaking slowly and in a very quiet voice…

"Where are we"?

Lara is speechless. Absolutely speechless. If she had tried to speak she would have made no sense to Sarah, herself, nor anyone else.

"Again, Lara, where are we"? asked Sarah even more quietly as if speaking too loudly was a crime with a punishment of death here. Sarah was driving about 5mph and staring out the window at everything in amazement. Lara was gobsmacked even more than she was by her shared alien abduction. But rather like Alice who found herself in Wonderland, she gained her composure and old fashioned pre-Disclosure rational mind that people had not grown out of when it came to experiences like this one.

"Sarah, I do not think the most important question is 'where are we? I think the most important question is 'when are we'?

Sarah wound her side door window down. People were staring at Sarah and Lara and staring at the car like they were a freak show. Winding the window down made the two women consciously aware of the stench of horse manure. And the people were dressed in very old fashioned clothes. They heard British accents.

Sarah said I think I know where we are and I think I know approximately when we are. I think we are in London in Victorian times.

Lara said "We are driving a 21st century car. They'll mob us and do experiments on us. I would rather be caught by the greys. Drive, drive fast. NOW!"

And with that, Sarah drove at high speed through 1800s London. Sarah and Lara couldn't resist but stare at the people outside of their car. Men in top hats and tailcoats, women in long dresses and bonnets. Through the open window they could not only smell the horse manure everywhere, they could also see and hear the clip-clop of horses' hooves on cobblestones. They could hear a church bell tolling and a steam engine whistle blowing. Then the smell changed. With no modern sanitation systems in place, the city stank full of unpleasant odours from human waste to rotting food. Then they picked up a scent of coal smoke from a factory. They then saw the Houses of Parliament in the distance.

They came to a street that was almost empty of people. This gave Sarah much more confidence knowing that there was no chance of herself and Lara being captured for whatever reason that may happen. Sarah slowed the car down and shouted towards a woman walking along the pavement while holding the hand of her daughter. Sarah said "Excuse me. We are time-travellers from 2023. Do you know what year it is in your time?" Lara looked aghast whispering "Sarah, I'm not even sure if time travel existed as a concept for Victorians".

The Victorian looked at Sarah, and asked "What is that contraption?"

Sarah smiled and said mockingly "It's a car sweetheart".

Lara showed her disapproval at Sarah's comment by elbowing Sarah's arm while whispering "What are you doing?"

Sarah continued by asking the Victorian "Do you know where I can get wi-fi for my lap-top"? Sarah deliberately put on an expectant look on her face as if the Victorian might be able to help with that.

The Victorian looked at Sarah as she tried to work out what was going on here. But nothing came into mind.

Then Lara spoke up "Sorry, we are just lost. Sorry to bother you." Lara looks directly at Sarah, raises her voice and demands "DRIVE YOU IDIOT".

A-little fear and dis-trust surfaced into the mind of the Victorian woman. She found the whole encounter very odd. She turned around and walked (hand-in-hand with her child) in the opposite direction to create as much distance from Sarah, Lara and that contraption as she possibly could. She would later tell a neighbour of her encounter but her neighbour would be totally unable to shed any light on the experience for the bewildered Victorian woman.

"Oh happy days. That was fun" said Sarah. "I should have invited her to get in the car. We could have taken her back to 2023 with us… assuming we get back to 2023 that is".

Lara just looked at Sarah while mildly disapproving of her antics.

After a momentary pause Lara said "I'm normally the comedian. This is a bit of a role reversal"

"Not sure I know how we are going to live round here" said Sarah to Lara, still making jokey comments. "They won't take dollars. You can't go online so no Youtube or twitter for you. They won't do internet banking, you can't get Netflix. How did these people live"?

"However I hear the theater is good" she continued.

"I think what we are going through is a better show than going to watch Macbeth. Besides we do not have the currency required to buy a theater ticket".

"We could get in. We will be rich and famous here. We could sell the car and claim to be time travelers" said Sarah only half jokingly.

"We are time travelers" responded Lara who was also thinking of proving it by predicting future events while here.

"This could still all be simulated somehow" Sarah responded not letting go of her theory and getting serious-minded again. "And don't forget" she continued, "our street turning into a beach was temporary".

"Oh I think that guy, what's his name, Masters is onto something now with his time travel theory".

Sarah argued her own logic, which wasn't so sure about what Lara had just said about Masters. "Yeah, but surface appearances remember. When abducted by aliens you and most people think its ET. Although I admit when the environment just changes from a street to a beach I think its human simulation".

"Look I know what this all is. It's a f*****g MIRACLE" shouted Lara.

"Anyway, where are we driving too?"

"I'm trying to find H.G. Wells. Where do you think, I don't know. I haven't been to Victorian England for quite a while. Maybe we have to follow a yellow brick road or something".

"The Others have one weird sense of humour" said Lara just before Sarah turned a corner and the whole world changed once more. But they hadn't followed a yellow brick road back to Boston. Instead they were now aboard a UFO with grey aliens staring at them out of those huge almond shaped eyes. One of them telepathically spoke to the two women.

"It's time you learned about consciousness".

Perhaps the Grey was rather cheeky for saying its time you learned about consciousness to a psychiatrist.

The grey continued "You must learn to control the environment with your mind".

Sarah and Lara, feeling rather like the Victorian woman felt, say nothing.

The grey continues "Control this craft with your mind".

"Have you got a death wish!" replied Lara, who then added...

"Is it a literal UFO craft"?

"It is a UFO craft because we think it is a UFO craft. Everything you think of as reality is only so because you think it is so".

Lara looks at Sarah and asks "Did I take DMT earlier"?

Sarah isn't sure if Lara's question was serious or a joke. But she thought that DMT couldn't create a world more crazy than the one she was experiencing right now. Last year's Sarah would be sectioning this year's Sarah in a very secure facility for the mentally ill. Sarah then makes the point to the greys that neither she nor Lara thought the beach into reality nor did she or Lara think Victorian England into reality. The grey responds by telepathically communicating to them that the aliens are trying to open humans minds up so that they can know that thought = reality. Once humans genuinely think they can control the environment with their mind then they evolve to the next stage.

"Knowing that you can control the craft with the mind is a step along the path to knowing that you can control your environment and so-called reality with the mind".

"Which UFO researcher is closest to being right about the Phenomenon?" asks Lara.

"Probably Nolan and Vallee. But each of the theorists you look into seems to be a-bit right. You experience a Simulation and time is like a CD… all existing at once.

But physical science is old hat. You can think your way into the past or future. Thought = reality. Meanwhile we greys are real but we only nudge you along the path. But Simulation, ET's, time-travel, the paranormal are all true in a way".

Maybe the Greys were meaning a consciousness type of simulation.

"What about our Governments and the cover-up"? asks Lara.

"Your governments didn't know the answers but they knew it was happening and they knew it was an intelligence that could be generally termed the 'Others' doing this. Your governments have been too needy for power. This has been the way humans have been for millennia but that changes now".

"Are we like flies compared to you in terms of intelligence"? asks Sarah who asks the question even though she is convinced the answer is yes.

"You see that's why we don't fly craft over New York, London, Paris, Milan during peak times. We do not believe in being worshipped as gods. We think that we are all just consciousness with the same potentialities. Humans merely need to switch their focus, switch their attention".

Sarah is totally freaked out by the experience but Lara feels more relaxed now. She looks at the grey they are communicating with and says "You know when I asked who is the closest to being right and you named Nolan and Vallee... well you could of said Grant Cameron right, because he has talked about abductees controlling the craft with their mind".

The alien looked into Lara's eyes and responded

"I can't understand Grant Cameron. He speaks too fast".

That reply was too much for Sarah. Grey aliens doing humor!?! She faints. The next thing she knows she is back home with Lara lying beside her. Their minds had been opened up sufficiently to understand that while they can never really understand the true nature of reality they did now understand that they had been living in a Narrative Matrix. Whether there was also a technologically Simulated or Consciousness Matrix they may never know for sure. But they considered their minds to be ultra open. These two women were open to the idea that Sarah's car was somewhere in 1800s London. It doesn't get more open-minded than that.

Chapter 3: Lara: The Flawed Genius

Lara woke up with a fright. Images, emotions and incomplete thoughts swirled through her head. Images of Greys and disc shaped UFOs. Emotional excitement, fear, intrique. And thoughts of the relativisation of reality. F**k thought Lara. I wasn't abducted again was I? She glanced at Sarah laying beside her. Sarah was asleep and undisturbed. Lara walked over to a window, obsessing about being abducted. Obsessing about the transformation of her life, her reality, about the very experience of being a human being in the Post Disclosure World. UFO reality (of some sort or other) was now considered mainstream. The reality of the exotic nature of them was accepted. Millions of people had been abducted. Nevertheless it was still miraculous to many people as everyone could still recall the pre-Disclosure world when it seemed that the typical person could go through their entire life without ever thinking or feeling deeply about UFO's. Now it was almost all anyone could think about. Sarah and Lara had experienced more than most. They had experienced shared abductions, the street that Sarah lives on suddenly transforming into a beach and while driving in current day northeastern United States suddenly finding themselves driving in the same car in Victorian London, where supposedly the car still is. Sarah had originally felt the more psychologically impacted by these miracles but as time went by, that honor switched to Lara. Lara thought so much about the UFO Phenomenon that it was overwhelming her. She wanted her brain to slow down and for it to distract itself from itself. Lara's brain isn't slowing down right now. She's unable to sleep and therefore getting up ridiculously early. This wakes Sarah up. It feels like the middle of the night to Sarah and she isn't surprised to see a digital clock showing it to be just after quarter past four. She rolls over murmuring "Toooo early"

"Yeah well my brain is evolving fast and I can't sleep" replies Lara.

That comment peaks Sarah's interest. She responds

"That's the most egotistical insomnia I have ever heard and I'm a mental health professional"

"But it's not my ego. Nor was it a joke. It's connected to my contact experiences".

"You mean your abductions"?

"Yes. They dominate my dreams and all the hours I am awake".

Sarah yawns and says "My dreams are Freudian wish fulfilment dreams". She closes her eyes.

Sarah might have been very interested in what Lara was saying given her profession and the fact that this is her wife saying these things. But she is too tired to keep the conversation going and drifts off back to sleep. Sarah's dreams are more pleasant than Lara's. She dreams of being back at the lakeside holiday house with Lara. Nevertheless, just before she blissfully fell back asleep she made a mental note of Lara's insomnia.

Sarah gets up 4 hours later than Lara. Its a weekend so no work for the psychotherapist. She walks in on Lara on her laptop. Sarah is puzzled to see her checking out a friendly match between Argentina and Brazil.

"I didn't know you were interested in soccer".

"I'm not".

"So why are you engrossed in that Web page"?

"If you must know, I am placing a bet on Argentina to beat Brazil and Messi to score".

"Gambling. Don't get too much into that. You should see some of the penniless cases we receive at the institute. Some of them are on the verge of committing suicide".

"Do they really kill themselves over losing bets"?

"They chase their losses and lose more and more. Its the downward spiral that destroys them. Most go as far as developing suicidal thoughts. A minority actually put those thoughts into practice. The point is all of them are in a terrible place psychologically. I have seen and heard enough to despise betting companies".

"Those poor bastards. And shit, how do you stay sane yourself Sarah?"

Sarah smiles, approaches Lara and says "Why, that would be you" before kissing Lara's smiling lips.

Sarah leaves the room, and Lara places her bet. It is true she is not into soccer and this bet was to distract her from thoughts and imagery entering her head, seemingly from the outside. She even bet $50... which was much more than she originally planned. This she did despite Sarah's words... done in order to focus her mind on the match rather than on the bombardment of her brain from all things UFO related.

Later that day, Brazil ran out 2–0 winners thus Lara lost her bet. Lara reacted with one word: "F**k!". But this time Sarah had done well. Because Lara seriously considered chasing her loss but she could still hear Sarah's words on that. Had Sarah not said what she did, Lara would have started to go down the gambling rabbit hole at this point. But she resisted doing so. That particular rabbit hole would come a little later.

It was evening time now and Lara was actually buzzing.

"Sarah, I'm telling you now that its a Simulation of some sort".

"Great. But how do you know that???"

"Well… err… this is going to sound hard to believe but…"

"Spit it out Lara. Its me, Sarah. I know you wouldn't make up BS to me".

"Ok, well you know Jim Penniston had a download… the binary code thing… well I have similarly been given an upgrade".

"And the upgrade tells you its a Simulation? What, like you hear a voice saying humans live in a Simulation"?

"No, not exactly. Its images and feelings that are translatable" replied Lara who had actually started to hear words but not anything amounting to much. Hence her answer to Sarah was designed to not complicate things.

"Are those images and feelings crystal clear"?

"Its a bombardment of images, feelings… they become quite clear after a while due to the similarity of them… all telling me the same thing".

"Its a shame they didn't show you images of Brazil scoring two goals".

Lara eye rolls and asks "Yeah, but you believe me on the Simulation stuff right"?

"Yes, actually I do. Its not that difficult for me to do so to be honest. Those abductions, the changing of our street into a beach, the 1800s London thing. I'm your wife but if you were a mere acquaintance and we went through that stuff together I would find it easy to believe you".

"That's good to know. There's another thing though. The simulations imagery is not just from our time. Far from it. Its from ALL TIMES."

Sarah thought for a moment and then said… "Yeah, that sounds right. We were in Victorian London… simulated London. It was certainly time travel. And the street come beach experience smacks of simulated universe".

"Yes, Yes, Yes. But its overwhelming me".

"In what way?"

"Thought intrusion or external stuff taking over my mind… feeling I have no choice but to experience a bombardment of mental phenomena entering my head".

"Wow. You might require hypnosis Lara".

"Nah. Nothing will stop this"… said Lara suddenly impacted by what most people would call Grey alien imagery. Sarah observes that Lara seems disturbed by something.

"What's wrong Lara"?

"You know the Greys... they are not aliens. They are us in the future. They are the simulators of space and the time-travelers... and they are human. They are interested in us because they are us. They are operating a Control System."

Sarah listened intensely as Lara continued...

"Less than 100 people in our time are aware of the whole picture. I think its as little as 10–30 people. Its so compartmentalized. And besides, its the future humans that are in charge. They leave us craft that we call crash retrievals but they weren't accidentally crashed. They are purposely left for us. This is done to level us up. A slower version of what they have done to me. And clearly they are speeding things up on a global scale now with the abductions of millions of people which has propelled us into a Post Disclosure World. But humanity only knows that there are Others who are more intelligent than us. So they know a-lot but they definitely do not possess the complete picture. I DO".

Sarah pondered what she had heard for a moment before saying "This is intense. I don't know whether I should respond as a psychotherapist, as your wife or to simply react with awe that I have just heard the person I am closest to inform me that she has cracked the ultimate nature of reality"!

"I wish I hadn't".

"And that is because these images and so forth that enter your mind feel like they are from an external source so you feel like you are losing your psychological freedom"?

"Exactly".

"Try and relax. Pour yourself a glass of that Gibson Martini you bought yourself the other day. Then have a good nights sleep".

Lara did just that. Unbeknown to Sarah she didn't just buy the one bottle of Gibson Martini. She had a secret stash of bottles of Gibson Martini's hidden away from Sarah's prying eyes.

It was Monday morning and Sarah headed off to work leaving Lara alone with her own (or should that be the others) thoughts whirling around her head. She had an urge to write about it all. Was this because she is a writer or because it is coming from the outside? She answered herself with two words "the latter"! Indeed, she had already written quite a-lot in this regard. And that brought about resistance. Because Lara felt like she was being told to think and write about this regardless of what she wanted to do. As a writer of fiction she suddenly thought about the writer, Paul Sheldon, in Stephen King's Misery and felt some empathy with the fictional Sheldon. She considered the attackers of her mind as playing the role of Annie Wilkes. The urge to conform to the attack on her mind was so powerful. But she decided to fight back. It was only 10.30am but she had already had enough of these unrelenting attacks on her minds freedom. She went to her gym sports-bag and removed a bottle of her secret stash of Gibson Martini. She then walked to the kitchen and poured herself a large glass before entering the main front room of the house and putting on the Pointer Sisters upbeat track, I'm so Excited. She ensured the volume was full blast and started singing and dancing along to it. She then put on Elton John's Crocodile Rock, returning with a bottle of Chardonnay Wine. She didn't bother pouring it into a glass. She sang and danced along to it while drinking from the bottle. She was drinking too early, too fast and being totally stupid. If Sarah could see Lara now she would be shocked and upset. Lara was mixing her drinks, and it wasn't 11am yet. And she wasn't finished. In Lara's head this was working. The UFO stuff had been nuked from her brain. All she could hear was crocodile rock. The song ended and she was already light headed. She had downed a large Gibson and almost half a bottle of chardonnay already. Lara laughed and said "Jesus". She continued like this until finally she collapsed while drinking and singing along to Meat Loafs Dead Ringer for Love.She was unconscious and had collapsed onto a table scattering her writings on Simulation, Time-Travel and the Greys all over the place. So Lara was unconscious, some of her written notes were still on the table, some had fell to the floor on and near to Lara, and there were bottles of empty and (in one case) near empty alcohol bottles near to her as well. Lara started to regain consciousness when disaster struck. Sarah had come home just after 12 mid-day for a short break and bite to eat. She entered the front room and surveyed the scene. She whispered

"What the f**k!"

Lara didn't even bother to defend herself. Instead tears entered her eyes as she muttered "no no no no". She was trying to deny the reality of Sarah coming home and seeing what she was now seeing. Sarah continued to stare at the scene. Lara continued to expect a verbal onslaught. But instead Sarah stormed out of her own house and went back to work. Normally Lara would try and stop her but she was well aware that she couldn't even walk straight. So her only response was to sit up and vomit all over the floor.

As Sarah was driving back to work her thoughts were all over the place too. She was upset and angry. Lara had opened up to her to some extent but obviously the problem was far worse. Sarah parked outside the Boston Mental

Health Institute (where she worked), deliberately banged her head against the steering wheel three times and then blasted the car horn 3 times while tears welled up in her eyes. In her head she was thinking For f**ks sake, I don't want to be with someone who solves their problems like a 20 year old student!!! However, Sarah was also aware of the magnitude of discovery that Lara was making. Hence, this enabled her to forgive her on one condition. She would warn Lara that if this ever happened again their relationship was over irrespective of her wife's cosmic discoveries.

Sarah was now in the mindset of looking back at happier times. She didn't think that the current problems were the type that could be switched off like a light switch or would just go away after a few days. She did not think her profession made it possible for her to analyze this away. She was fully aware that exotic Others existed having experienced so much of this new world herself. But she was very worried and not too optimistic about the foreseeable future. She didn't need to be asleep to dream and long for what she had experienced in the past such as the Lakeside House, its beautiful surrounding environment, and the company of a healthy Lara.

When Sarah got home that night she told Lara who was bedridden from all of the alcohol intake that she was forgiven for the earlier madness. However "you must make sure that your work and your relationship with me beat these demons inside of you otherwise I will not be so forgiving next time around".

Lara was feeling too sick to promise anything. Sarah understood this and said that they'll talk properly when the inevitable "huge hangover" is over.

Tuesday evening and the two women are sat on the corners of their bed upstairs with Lara ready to talk.

"Sorry."

"hhmmm, I hope so, if you are becoming an addict then there's a high chance you will relapse".

"I won't"

"hhmmm"

"Well, what can I say to help?"

"I am not saying you will relapse. I am saying you will have to be strong. So promise you will be strong when the urge to go back on your word enters your consciousness".

"I promise".

"Hey" says Sarah.

"what?"

"I suppose that given that the Others are humans from the future they will not be at all surprised at your response to mind controlling you. I could never get my head around what aliens would think about us and that made them hard to believe in. But future humans know all about us because they are us."

"You would think they would choose someone better than myself for this task"

"I was thinking something similar. Why didn't they choose me?"

"Maybe they wanted it to be more fun!"

"Alright, alright. But you won't be able to mend our relationship with time-travel. You cannot actually travel back in time. So its important that you keep some guilt in mind to keep you on your toes. When those thoughts outside of yourself enter your head again… come to me… even if I'm at work".

Lara thought to herself that those external feelings, thoughts, images are almost always in her head. But she did not feel in a position to challenge Sarah.

"Ok will do. So no in-depth psychoanalysis from the shrink then?"

"I think a mix of understanding, warning, and if you relapse, tough love is what you need."

"But we would be finished so isn't that tougher than tough love?"

"If you did that level of drinking again during the morning, collapsing and throwing up then I would have no choice but to kick you out. But I love you so if you completely turned yourself around I would consider letting you off one last time. But it would be very painful so just stay dry. But yeah, no in-depth psychoanalysis other than to say I would also want you to confess your condition."

"Well, I suppose I know where I stand then. That is very clear. I can see the potential future if I go wrong almost as if I had a time machine".

"Stay sensible Lara. Or at least not stupid. Get some rest. I'm going to pour myself a small wine then I will join you. But you are going to go to sleep. Night Night".

Lara felt lucky to be in the same bed as her wife given that she could have potentially been kicked out of the entire house. She drifted off to sleep. Her dreams were full of thoughts, ideas, concepts… this invasion from the outside into the former privacy of her own mind were trying to give her ideas concerning how to express and articulate the nature of reality. When she woke up she had a light bulb moment. The future humans didn't choose someone like a Quantum Physicist because they thought that a story teller would express the message they want to get across in language that the masses understand. And yes, Lara was preferred by the future humans relative to Sarah, on similar grounds.

The next morning Lara told Sarah that she was now hearing voices and they are telling her that once she has written out the truth concerning the nature of reality the voices inside her head want her to go public. Sarah responded that it wasn't long ago she would have believed that her wife was suffering from schizophrenia. But not anymore. However, Sarah was worried sick as she did not think it was fair that the ultimate responsibility was on Lara's shoulders. The point about having to go public on what the UFO Phenomenon's answers were was something Sarah wanted Lara to reject. At this point in time Lara agreed with Sarah on this point. But the more Lara resisted the more that the future humans bombarded Lara's head.

"I bet you believe in the goodness of individual agency now Lara" said Sarah only 25% jokingly!

"Yes. This is mind possession. Are future humans unethical or something!!!"

"I wish this was a mental condition. I would have a much better idea of what to do to help you. But I am not delusional. I can't take on future humans who are accessing your brain at will".

Sarah went to work and Lara started to cry. Lara's resistance to going public on this were being met with voices telling her that she has no choice. She MUST go public. The future humans were telling Lara that she is the chosen one which was a burden Lara did not want. She never dreamed of being an historical figure.

Lara wondered about her choices. Would the images and voices go quiet if she just started to work on outlining what she knows, typing and printing it out? Or do these voices want her to genuinely commit to going public? Its like they do not just insert thoughts, images and feelings into Lara's mind... they also read her mind. Even if she wanted to, it is highly doubtful that she would know how to go public. Other choices that she considered in terms of silencing the mind possessing included getting totally drunk again or perhaps scaring her mind with a huge bet would do the trick. The healthiest answer would have been to work and to promise to go public with bucket loads of help from the future humans. She thought that the future humans were convinced she is qualified in succeeding on this task. But Lara did not think she was the right choice overall due to not knowing how to go public. She thought that it would require powerful connections in the news media and she knows no one in that regard. Nevertheless working on the issues concerning the nature of reality with an open mind to going public would have quietened the mind possession and not had any other negative impact on her health. But Lara made unhealthy choices. She opted to gamble. $300 on Barcelona to beat Real Madrid in the Spanish Cup being played that night. Her intention was to make herself nervous. However, it turned out that it wasn't enough to quieten her mind. She joked to herself with the line… do I need to attain Buddhist nirvana or something???? She couldn't be much further away from such an attainment right now as she grabbed a bottle of Chardonnay from the fridge and played Venus by Shocking Blue full blast. No sooner did she start downing the wine straight from the bottle than she heard Sarah pull up in the car. "F*****G HELL" shouted Lara, her heart beating fast. She had to think fast. She ran to the kitchen with the Chardonnay and put it back in the fridge. She then went back to the front room and switched off the music. Sarah entered the house. Luckily she had got away with near disaster. Indeed, had Sarah not come back it is likely that Lara would have messed up as badly as last time around. Infact it would have been all the worse given that it would have been a second time. It would have played havoc with her relationship with Sarah and the future humans would have simply increased the noise in her head after she had recovered from her hangover.

"I came back to see you are alright."

Lara was relieved. She had nearly lost her mind. But it wasn't all her fault.

Lara looked into Sarah's eyes. She walked up to her and declared "I must write". She said that in such a serious tone of voice that it slightly unnerved Sarah.

My wife is possessed said Sarah to herself.

Lara then walked back into the front room and spent the next 2 and a half hours writing a draft paper explaining that what has happened to the world in recent times equates to a discovery of human time-travelers that want us to know about their presence. They are also simulators who play with reality like a toy. And the greys are therefore not extraterrestrial. They are future humans. She was especially interested in analyzing what she thinks Michael Masters has got right and wrong in his book that advocates the future humans hypothesis as the answer to the questions surrounding the origins of UFO's and the greys. Lara regarded her own convictions as proven to herself and beyond hypothesis and she added that the greys can possess minds. She explained that is exactly how it is that she knows about all of this. Lara then thought to herself that the future humans will have to help her out here because there is no reason why the entire world should believe her on all of this. Christ, she hadn't been certain that Sarah would believe her.

Lara's brain was on fire. She started critiquing Jacques Vallee and penned that he is correct on the Control Theory although Lara discussed it as a certainty in terms of simulating environments for humans in the same way that dog lovers would simulate a VR environment for their pet dog that suited their nature. And she revised Carl Jung's and Wolfgang Pauli's synchronicity theory. She wrote that Synchronicities are caused by the time traveling simulators. She wondered if anyone will believe her? The good news here is that almost as soon as she wondered about the issue of the public believing her, her brain just seemed to tell her that the future humans would help her out on that score. Lara then jokingly asked the voices in her head "Can you help me out with my gambling? I should have an advantage due to being possessed by time travelers". Unfortunately there was no-response to that question.

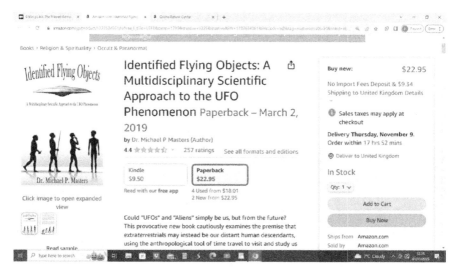

Lara critically analyzed Michael Masters text as part of her paper on the Greys & UFO's as simulators and human time travelers.

Lara revised Jung/Pauli's Synchronicity concept.

Lara had done well. Her work and increased openness (or at least acceptance) of perhaps having to go public, quietened the invading forces in her head.

Unfortunately her bet went down with Real Madrid winning 3–2 away to Barcelona. So her head wasn't totally at rest. She regretted the bet and repetitive thoughts of her own kept reminding herself of that fact. Indeed the Barcelona/Real Madrid result had made her thirst for success of her own. She was changing her mind about her future. Becoming an historical figure was now becoming enticing. It would render the monetary losses irrelevant as surely the glory of becoming a living legend would make her rich beyond her wildest dreams.

Lara penned a 33,000 word paper answering the questions that even this Post-Disclosure world still needed answering. The key question of course was 'Who are the

Others?' Answer = they are the Simulators of our world. 'Why are they interested in us'? Answer = Because they are us… they are future humans.

But now the part that Lara found much more daunting. With no connections inside the news media she somehow had to get a public profile through them. They must come to accept all of this as the truth. She sent her paper to CNN, Fox News, the New York Times, the Boston Globe, and to about 40 other news media organisations. Then she waited for the response. 3 days went by and nothing. Sarah said it was early days but Lara thought that someone would have got in-touch with her considering this is the biggest story in history. And now there was radio silence in her head. Ironically this irritated the living hell out of Lara who felt that the future humans owed her clarity on the predicament she found herself in.

"They all think I am an attention seeker and glory seeker" complained Lara, who had seemingly become more accurate concerning what had happened to her. Rather than being upgraded, fututre humans were actually in one way communication with her. And she was receiving the contact more clearly the more time went by.

"Well I remain quietly optimistic" replied Sarah, which wasn't really how Sarah felt. In truth she was inconsistent on what she thought was going on as this was all Alice in Wonderland territory. And yet somehow possibly true but maybe not. At this moment in time she thought that Lara was telling the truth as she sees it but her experience wasn't quite accurate. Nevertheless not for one second did Sarah think that Lara was mentally ill. She was consistently honest when saying that much to Lara.

The silence inside her head, her restoration of individual agency was not the relief that Lara had hoped for. Now she was accusing herself of mental illness. Had she gone through all of this for nothing? Was she insane? She panicked and went online finding as many news media organisations from around the world as she possibly could. And she sent her paper to all of them. Lara considered her action of sending off her paper to even more news networks as the same psychology as when she gets desperate involving betting and chases the bet. And just like she received no glory with the bookmakers, she received Al-zippo from the news media networks.

A week went by and still nothing from the news media. This despite the fact that Lara kept finding more and more news media sites online. She felt like she had covered the entire modern world's news media. And she felt increasingly like an idiot. She was hitting the drink and gambling again. She was $584 down on the gambling and had made the mistake of chasing her losses. She was less confident than ever that she was about to become a millionaire as a result of world-wide fame. Sarah was becoming more miserable herself as she felt like she was losing the Lara she used to know. Sarah didn't know about the gambling but she could see that she was obsessive.

Lara's gambling addiction was taking hold. But this did not just mean gambling money. She now felt like she had nothing to lose and was now willing to risk her marriage.

She was making bad choices. She was losing money and potentially losing Sarah all because she lost her mind's agency. Sarah's supportive words counted for little in this context. With nothing to lose and on one weekend she went to her secret stash, pulled out a Gibson Martini, put Venus on full volume, and started dancing infront of Sarah. With it being 7pm Sarah wasn't sure how to take this. But thoughts of her work colleagues (who she had confided in) came to mind.

"Am I going to be asking one of them to talk to Lara?" thought Sarah to herself.

"Is this you being happy or is this you regressing?" asked Sarah.

"Shush your cake hole. Sing and dance with me instead."

"I can't sing with my cake hole shut silly."

Every time the lyrics "Your Desire" were sung, Lara would point at Sarah with a fully outstretched arm.

Sarah was not fully into it and said "Your paper, I have read every word. It is pure genius."

Lara ignored her and continued prancing around the room and drinking rather fast.

"Ok ok ok. I will go along with this but no relapsing alright?"

"YOUR DESIRE!"

2 hours passed and Sarah was becoming suspicious as hell that this was not the normal Lara. And alcohol was starting to make Lara loose tongued.

"Oh I know what song to play now" said Lara ridiculously excitedly. Seconds later Frank Sinatra and Celeste Holm were at full blast singing Who wants to be a Millionaire? And that was the point where alcohol made Lara to stupidly honest as she said "Well that won't be us Sarah… we won't be millionaires. You wouldn't believe how much I have lost in gambling recently, almost $600". Lara then took a swig of Chardonnay from the bottle. Sarah moved away from her, sat down and put her head in her hands. When the song finished Lara said she loves that song so she played it again and moved towards Sarah while singing along to it in Sarah's face "Who wants to be a millionaire? I don't. Have flashy flunky's everywhere? I don't. Who wants the bother of a country estate. A country estate is something I'd hate. Who want's to wallow in champagne" Lara then changes the lyrics from 'I don't' to 'YES PLEASE". And a moment later when Lara sang "I don't, because all I want is you" Sarah's eyes welled up with tears. She gets up and walks out of the room. Lara carries on singing and prancing around the room. At this moment in time she is relatively drunk and has given up on life.

And Sarah is relatively sober and has given up on Lara. Lara prances out the room and points her finger right infront of Sarah's face and shouts "YOUR DESIRE"!!! Sarah shouts "GIVE IT A REST LARA. YOU ARE DRUNK, GAMBLING, AND DESTROYING OUR RELATIONSHIP! I WARNED YOU ABOUT THIS. YOU LEAVE TOMORROW AND IF YOU DON'T BECOME THE LARA I KNOW AND LOVE THEN WE ARE FINISHED. BUT I DON'T WANT A RELATIONSHIP WITH ONE OF MY ILL PATIENTS. AND YOU ARE COMING ACROSS LIKE ONE OF THEM".

"You are being so lame Sarah. I'm a GENIUS remember. You said it yourself. A GENIUUUSSS!!!" She goes into the front room and plays the Marcels Blue Moon at full blast and goes back to Sarah singing infront of her face and tries to get her to dance or prance with her. Sarah responds by picking up Lara's drink and throwing it in her face.

Lara laughs while alcohol flows down her face.

"You egotistical prat" shouts Sarah. All you want is glory for your own ego. Its all about you isn't it. You want to be the new Albert Einstein or something. You are closer to being one of my clients by a long long long way."

"I am so hot for you right now" replies Lara.

Sarah was failing to get Lara to take any of this seriously. But tomorrow morning she would wake up with a hangover, regret about what she said and how she acted last night, and raging anxiety about her gambling addiction, and concerns about being an addict in general. She would worry about losing Sarah and wonder if she is going insane.

At 8am that next morning Sarah walked over to a sleeping Lara and said "GET UP. You are acting like a 20 year old student at best. But they aren't addicts. So you are worse. GET UP AND GET OUT"!

Lara started to cry. She protested for a bit saying "but we love each other" and "we have been through so much." She protested that this isn't her fault. But without the arrogance that alcohol provided Lara with…Sarah easily had the upper hand… so Lara did what she knew she had to do… and that was simply to get up and get out. Sarah desperately hoped she would get the old Lara back but she was far from sure that she would because Lara was a complete mess. The second that Lara shut the house door behind her, Sarah collapsed to the ground, her back falling back on the door, and she burst into tears.

For the next 5 days Lara stayed at her mothers house, acting like she was physically rather than just psychologically ill, spending most of the time in bed. And then on the 6th day she received a phone call from Sarah.

"Have you seen the news?" she asked.

"No" replied Lara, her lip trembling and tears pouring down her face as she heard the voice of the woman she longed to be with again.

"Let me take my phone to the news Channel, CNN, that is on right now". As Sarah did so, Lara heard the news reporter talking about a paper written by someone called Lara Hine which has been downloaded online over 1,750,000 times over night. It had been downloaded from Lara's own website and someone somewhere within the news media had noticed this.

Lara burst into tears. And Sarah was crying a-little too.

"Where are you right now?"

"I'm at my mothers."

"Stay there. I will come to you so we can compose ourselves, get our confidence and happiness back".

"Thank you" said Lara in floods of tears.

"I love you" continued Lara.

"I love you too."

As Sarah put the phone down she heard a great deal of noise from outside. She looked out the window and saw far more press than she expected. She quickly gathered some belongings, grabbed car keys and opened the door.

"LARA" a reporter shouted.

Sarah ignored them as other reporters said they don't think that is Lara. She walked past reporters who at least refrained from physically grabbing her, and she got into her car, speeding off as cameramen risked their lives standing in-front of her moving car. Sarah blasted the car horn and they dispersed. Seconds earlier Sarah was thinking to herself that it was lucky Lara wasn't here as all the press outside would have kept her imprisoned inside the house. But she changed her mind the second she saw the press following her in their car. They will surely just gather outside her mothers house instead. She phoned Lara again and informed her of the situation. Much to her surprise Lara told Sarah to drive nice and slowly so as to let them follow her to her mothers house. Driving slowly, Lara explained, would also give her time to be ready for them and to prepare her historical speech. Then Lara said

"Drive them a minute from my mothers house and then stop the car and get out of it. When the reporters get out of their cars tell them that I want to deliver a statement that will go down in history. The press are free to gather outside the house but I do not want to be inundated with questions at this point. If they agree tell them that you will drive them to the door".

"Are you sure about all of this?"

"Never more sure about anything before in my life. And I want you stood by me as I make the statement"

"It will be an honor."

The Statement

"Good afternoon, ladies and gentlemen of the press. My name is Lara Hine. Today, I stand before you to share an extraordinary revelation that has been bestowed upon me by beings from the future. These beings, who identify themselves as future humans, have communicated with me and provided insights into the mysterious abductions that have plagued humanity recently.

According to these future humans, it is they who have been responsible for the abductions that many have attributed to extraterrestrial beings. These beings assert that our reality is nothing more than a simulation, and through these abductions, they sought to demonstrate this fact by altering our so-called physical environment. We experience what they want us to experience as they are operating a simulated Control System. Many of you will be familiar with the term 'Control System' thanks to the work of Jacques Vallee. They are also responsible for synchronicities.

Furthermore, the future humans reveal that what we commonly refer to as 'grey aliens' are actually our own evolved form. Over time, they explain, humanity will undergo significant changes in physiology and appearance due to advancements in technology and evolution. These changes will result in the emergence of these 'grey aliens,' who are essentially our own descendants.

The paper I wrote detailing these encounters has been downloaded an astounding 1,750,000 times. Given that it had created absolutely no interest for weeks I am certain that it is the future humans themselves that have been involved in some way in the downloads… they are almost certainly the downloaders themselves.

I understand why you in the press ignored my paper. Ever since we entered the Post-Disclosure World there has been thousands or millions of people trying to cash in, make up stories as they seek attention and glory. But I assure you that my intentions are sincere. The future humans have chosen me as a conduit to deliver this message, and it is my duty to share it with the world.

I urge the media and scientific community to approach this revelation with an open mind. Let us embark on a journey of exploration and discovery, seeking to understand the nature of our reality and the potential implications of these revelations. Together, we can unravel the mysteries that have eluded us for so long. From this moment humanity accepts what impacts us as a miracle. I am honored to have been chosen as the person to deliver this message. And I hope that we can now experience open contact with our future selves.

Thank you."

The Irony... and a potential Twist?

Sarah headed off to the betting shop, skipping down the street while singing Who wants to be a Millionaire and changing the lyrics to "I DO"... as she had bet $200 on the discovery of human time travelers at odds of 5000 to 1.

But has all of this been the most bizarre and elaborate Psy-Op in the history of the human race?

Chapter 4: Lara and the Psy-Op

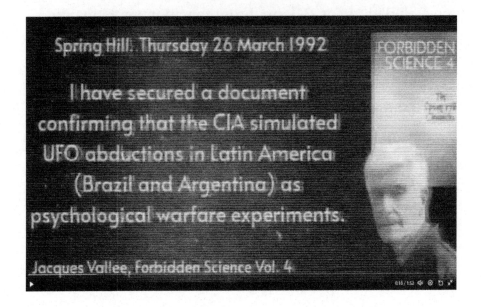

Spring Hill. Thursday 26 March 1992

I have secured a document confirming that the CIA simulated UFO abductions in Latin America (Brazil and Argentina) as psychological warfare experiments.

Jacques Vallee, Forbidden Science Vol. 4

Sarah Aston has achieved her dream of living and being with Lara Hine, seemingly forever at her beloved Lakeside House away from the hustle and bustle of Boston's city life. The two women are now very rich due to two reasons:

Lara on the Lecture Circuit and Selling her Story to the Press. She of course is the woman who answered the 'Who are they?' question concerning the intelligence behind the

UFO craft. She had discovered that they are humans from the future and that they simulate our so called physical environment.

Sarah's winning bet on the discovery of human time travelers.

But Lara had been keeping a mind-blowing secret from Sarah. Everything she had said recently about time travelers, about her communication with time travelers, about simulation, about being a genius in any shape-or-form, and everything about being an addict in any shape-or-form had been lies and an act. So yes, she certainly did get drunk and throw up and put on a great show in the process. The tears, the addictions, were all an act. Yes, she had too much to drink and she gambled but these were to convince Sarah that she was an addict. It was all part of the plan. So for example, when she placed her first soccer bet on her lap-top she deliberately did it in plain sight, for Sarah to see that she was doing it. And when she blurted out that we won't be millionaires to Sarah due to how much she (Lara) has lost gambling, she pretended to say that because she was loose tongued due to alcohol consumption, but she had planned it that way. She made it look like alcohol had made her say it. She had been drunk but she was very aware of what she was doing. But why would Lara do this to Sarah? Because of two reasons:

So they could live happily ever after at the Lakeside House. And

2. Peace on Earth. Clearly Number 2 needs explaining. But first we need to clear up more deceit that occurred earlier during the Psy-Op.

The narrative was that millions of people had been abducted and that led to a Soft Disclosure that exotic unknown Others were carrying out the abductions. But the true figure was actually in the hundreds of thousands. Moreover the vast majority of those were people making false claims as they worked in the Deep State on the Psy-Op. They were the same people who also downloaded Lara's later 33,000 word paper. But what about Sarah's individual abductions that she experienced? They were Mi-

Labs abductions. MILAB stands for Military Abduction. The phenomenon was first investigated by Dr. Helmut Lammer of the Austrian Space Research Institute. In a number of cases abductees, and sometimes UFO witnesses, are subsequently abducted by humans in military uniforms. In Sarah's case they were disguised as Greys. They also carried out the simulating of the physical environment, e.g., Sarah and Lara suddenly finding themselves in Victorian London, and Sarah's street turning into a beach. These abductions were absolutely necessary for Sarah to become convinced of Lara's later claim to be being contacted by time travelers who simulate our so-called physical environment. Lara had also tried to open Sarah's mind with DMT so that she would more likely believe the later time traveler communications that Lara claimed she was experiencing.

Humans most certainly could simulate environments and distort reality but it was nothing to do with time travel. But the time travel lie was imperative for a huge reason. The Deep State believed that if they could convince the people that World War 3 (and other horrendous wars) had occurred in the foreseeable future and everyone had been a loser as a result of these wars, i.e., apocalypse all-round, countless deaths, major injuries, a bloodbath to end all bloodbaths, returning humanity to the Middle Ages, PTSD as the overwhelming norm… then they could create a world of peace and harmony, free from war. To this end they even paraded so-called figures from the future to talk and educate us about the horrors coming up in the near future that could be only avoided if (and only if) we came together as One Humanity. Those so-called Time Travelers lecturing us on future events were in reality, figures from the Deep State… the same figures instructing Lara and carrying out Mi-Lab Simulated abductions.

Everything was going perfectly as planned until the day that Lara told Sarah the truth.

So why on earth did Lara tell Sarah the truth?

Because she did this for the money and for peace. The money side of it was for her and Sarah to live happily ever after. The peace side of it she thought truly noble and worth putting heart and soul into the cause. But now, with it all done-and-dusted, Lara thought that she had to tell Sarah as they don't keep secrets. In Lara's mind this meant they don't keep unnecessary secrets. The problem is… when Sarah hears this, she thinks the human population also merit the truth and that shocks Lara who immediately regrets telling her the truth.

"You cannot tell anyone I have told you this Sarah. I have signed a Non-Disclosure Agreement, an NDA. I would go to prison"

"So you go to prison for doing your duty and telling the truth. You become a millionaire for lying to the world. The world truly is messed up. And the authorities you have been dealing with behind my back are even more messed up than you. But I won't tell anyone. It is your duty to tell the world the truth!"

"Ha Ha Ha Ha Ha … you cannot be serious!!!!"

"Its all a lie".

"Yeah, a noble lie that saves millions of lives"

"Saves millions of lives??? I don't think so. Saves us from a fake World War 3 more like!"

"Yeah but don't you see the point? Without this fake human time traveler psy-op World War 3 would eventually happen. So we have saved millions, even billions of lives."

"Who are you Lara? How the f**k did you pull this off?"

"Well it wasn't really my plan."

"Let's recall that you were scheming to win me from Mike. You possess the schemer gene. And, yeah, what about Mike, my ex husband? Did he really die in that car crash? Was his death part of the plan?"

"Yeah he did really die. But remember he was trying to kill us both. He had gone mad. But no, his death was not part of the plan. That was all real."

"So my car isn't in Victorian London, then?"

Lara laughed. Sarah didn't find the laugh funny.

"[laughing/giggling] No. It's not."

"So where is it?"

"Current day Boston Sarah." Lara tries to hold back further laughter.

"What made you think it was ok to give my car away?"

"The promise of being able to afford 10,000 cars in the near future."

"But the abductions of millions of people…"

"Never happened."

"What do you mean, we know it did. I saw people on TV."

"Yeah, there were a few Mi-Lab abductions by current day humans, not time-travelers. You experienced those. We experienced those. But they were probably about 30,000 abductions in major cities around the world. Then there were several hundred thousand figures from the Deep State presenting themselves as everyday Joe Bloggs and Jane Doe people, who completely made-up very convincing everyday people profiles, and completely made up stories about alien abduction. And they did this in an organised and simultaneous way. And it worked."

"You wrote a 33,000 word paper which can only be described as a work of fiction. And what about when you were checking out the UFO field? UFO twitter and all of that? Was all of that just an act?"

"I was actually getting into the UFO twitter stuff. And it was also necessary to gain knowledge. Slightly contributed to my paper but really, when you are saving the world then 33,000 words is nothing."

"You are simply a short story writer so 33,000 words must have seemed like a lot. You are simply a short story writer yet they made you their choice for this cosmic scam. No wait. You could be much more. You could be an A-list movie actor. I mean the tears, the vomiting, the addict impression, the statement for the whole god-damn world to hear. F*****g Genius!"

"Thank you Sarah" Lara said laughing. She then adds

"And look we are rich from it all and the world is at peace. And think about what would happen to me if I came clean. I would be destroyed."

Sarah puts her head in her hands because the last point Lara made was undeniable. Sarah was now totally conflicted. On the one hand she thought that she and the entire human race had been scammed with her wife playing the leading role. On the other hand she did not want Lara to go down in history as the woman who lied to the world.

"You can see why I went along with it right? I couldn't tell you because if I did then you might have ran to the press."

Sarah still has her head in her hands and shouts "F**K! F**K! F**K"

Lara continues "The Simulation stuff is true. Isn't it amazing!!!"

"So they simulate Victorian London but we weren't actually in Simulated Victorian London?" replied Sarah.

"Your car is in Boston, United States of America Sarah. I promise you…" Lara laughs again.

"I remember when people all suddenly accepted the reality of UFOs and the Others. You reacted by praising sceptics because they didn't jump to the extraterrestrial hypothesis whereas believers tended to do so. You called the sceptics the "adults in the room." I guess that was because of the grand plan that you were involved in?"

"Absolutely, yes!"

"And that is why you were interested in Eric Weinstein's hypothesis?"

"Yes."

Sarah goes quiet, sees down at the dinner table and reflects back on a previous conversation she had with Lara... she recalls

Lara going online and showing her a tweet she found on one of her frequent UFO twitter searches. They were two pre-Disclosure tweets by the American cultural commentator, Eric Weinstein. In one of them he said that "we may be faking a UFO situation? Or that we may be covering up the duplicity of our own "Operation Fortitude" type program?" And he followed that tweet up by saying that it involves classified R & D, spying and deception. In that same tweet he said "something big is going on" but that he is not invested in "little green men".

Sarah recalls asking Lara "Does he still say that it's nothing to do with aliens now that we are past the old [pre Disclosure] world?"

Lara had answered "Yup".

"Ok, he might be onto something here".

Lara had explained… "Yeah, he thinks it's an attempt to create a New dominant myth on Planet earth. The UFO/ET Phenomenon as a cover for the U.S.' most advanced and exotic aerospace R&D".

"Geez, if true then this human clique take it really far with abduction simulations".

"Indeed. But it's worked hasn't it. And that is all the State Superstructure cares about."

Back in the present, Sarah says "The abductions, the abductors humor about not understanding a UFO researcher because he talks too fast… Christ… I should of, really should of…" She pauses because she was going to say she should have sussed it out. But no. She shakes her head and continues… "But the simulated environments are amazingly impressive. But my mind is swiss-cheesed right now. Because the world now has fake knowledge due to you."

"Well, as said it wasn't my plan. The idea for Psy-Op: The Advancement of Humanity came from…"

Sarah interrupted shouting "Oh I don't care Lara! It is well and truly f****d!"

"I hope WE are not."

"You can just get your Psy-Op mates to abduct me and mess with my mind. Are you planning on doing that to save your relationship and save the world from what I might blurt out?"

"Everything I did was for us and humanity".

"You keep telling yourself that. It will help you sleep at night."

"Beats the end of the human race becoming a thing. Can't we just agree to disagree?"

"This isn't just a disagreement on preference of apples and oranges."

"I know. It's a disagreement on life vs the apocalypse and its a disagreement on whether I go down in history as a genius or a fraud".

"So you are actually aware that you are one hell of a fraud? Did Genius Lara get anything wrong during the Grand Plan?"

"Yes I'm a fraud. But I'm a good person though, I have helped save billions of lives. Errmm I did get some things wrong-ish. At first if you recall I was to laid back and relaxed about being abducted. I don't think this was significant though. I found it easier to act messed up when I had the props of alcohol and declining dollars figures on my bank statements". Lara exaggeratingly places her finger on her lips and looks out of the corner of her eye at the ceiling. She then remarks, "I had a secret stash of alcohol in my Sports Bag. On more than once occasion I left the sports bag half unzipped for you to catch me out. And I did that at a time when I was supposed to be staying relatively or fully dry but you failed to notice. But it didn't really matter because I was on fire anyway. I think I am an exceptional actor as egotistical as that sounds. But I acted like an infiltrator of a terrorist group pretending to be on their side and passionate for their cause. I tried to play the role at all times, not only when you were home. The stuff about the time travelers dominating my thoughts was bullshit but on the other hand I was 24/7 obsessed with the Plan and at times a drink did help… but I didn't need to drink so much. Also I felt uneasy when you observed on a couple of occasions that I had referred to 'State Superstructure' which you considered out of character, so I binned that terminology. I wasn't 100% perfect. I thought that the riots that happened in the immediate aftermath of people realizing that something serious is going on might mean that things aren't going to plan but I was reassured with one phone call. I mean temporary riots are far preferable to World War 3. They are a price worth paying."

Sarah is sarcastically clapping… " Bravo, you truly bring the curtain down. What a performance. And you stayed in bed at your mothers house when I kicked you out. So you even went so far as to fool your own mother as well?"

"Absolutely. There's no way I could have told her. She would have had a heart attack. This is another reason why I can't come clean now."

"Huh! You miss the bigger picture. Humans are living a lie about the nature of reality. But I will give you this, you are a genius, not just in the way I thought you were. I mean, I never suspected a thing. The government were right to hire you. But you are a con-artist par excellence. But I mean it truly is genius. What about the patients we were inundated with who reported abductions, were they MILAB abductions?"

"Yes, they were. All to get you to believe me when we got to the time travel Psy-Op. Look its all a Psy-Op except my love of you. And yeah, before you interrupt, I do love the money as well. And we have peace on earth! But Sarah!!! We are going round in circles. You are just going to come back at me all the time with the fact that I have lied to the world, cosmic deceit, harmed knowledge, sent us back to mythology and so on. So let me put it like this. You are a Mental Health Professional. Well imagine how many people go to war and then come back with Post Traumatic Stress Disorder. I have prevented those countless people from going through that experience. As a Mental Health Professional you can surely appreciate the suffering that I have prevented."

"Ok! I admit conflict. My point isn't that I cannot see your point. My point is that I cannot think that what you did is all wonderful with no downside. I think what you did is to manipulate the human race and then cash in on it. AND you have saved people from suffering and I admit some of them probably prefer your decision to the alternative."

"I genuinely am absolutely delighted that war will not happen. The world is a better place. When I decided to go along with the plan I did ask myself if I would mind if you did this to me."

"Huh! So much for we tell each other everything. I want to throw up. Throwing up is something you did more than once recently during your genius Psy-Op. Did you force vomit to come out by shoving your finger down your throat or were you genuinely very drunk? And by the way, all of your work has sent the human race back to belief in myth. This aint science."

"Err, on the throwing up, I was definitely very drunk. Whats new on myth? Humans and Myth go together. You should know that due to Jung. However, be fair, the simulated environments part is new true knowledge."

Lara referring to Jung had triggered another memory in Sarah's mind.

"What about when you got me high? Was that part of the plan?"

"[Lara laughing again]. Yes! It was to open up your mind. You were far too stuffy serious Freudian for me. You had to become more Jung than Freud. You can go back to being Freudian now" Lara said giggling.

"I thought I was getting abducted by aliens. Why did I need DMT as well?"

"Because of what was coming later… me in contact with time travelers. I wanted you to be sure of things like a deep collective unconscious. Look, the more open your mind the better."

"No wonder you embraced the new reality far more quickly than I did. But aren't you conflicted at all about what you have done?"

"Nope. And sometimes I was sort of being genuine. I was once at our house while you were at work, just before the street turns into beach simulation and I was crying with happiness because this New World was going to be one of Peace."

"But you were lying to me. You deserve an Oscar. I didn't think you were capable of that."

"I did it for us."

Sarah goes silent and refuses to speak to Lara for the rest of the day. She is simply amazed at the absence of conflict within her wife's mind.

Lara Hine's public image was one of a genius and a Disclosure hero. There were statues up of her across the world. And yet in truth she possessed a You Cannot tell the People mindset. You cannot tell the people that we haven't really discovered time-traveling humans from the future. She viewed herself as a protector of the people, a hero for saving their lives, a hero for saving their mental health. She didn't inflate the hero too much, not psychologically anyway. But for those others who view conning the human race as inexcusable then Lara's image of herself would be irrelevant if they were made aware of the truth. Because for many people, knowingly conning the people on the nature of reality is as said, inexcusable. Lara was intelligent enough as a human being. But not surprisingly, given that she was not really a genius, she merely lied using a script that she repeated over-and-over again on the lecture circuit. But she had quickly given that up as she had grown fearful of being caught out concerning contradicting herself due to the press firing questions at her about knowledge given to her by the time travelers. She told reporters (and this was the truth) that she now wanted to go and live a blissful life with her wife and lover, Sarah Aston, at Sarah's Lakeside House. This also made her an LGBT icon of course.

Lara genuinely was not conflicted as she genuinely viewed all of this as good for humanity, good for her, and good for Sarah. She weighed up the lie vs the suffering if no lie told and thought the answer obvious. She continued to remind Sarah about the peace that had broke out, and the pleasant relations, between the likes of the U.S. and Russia, and U.S. and China. No one believed World War 3 would ever happen now. She also continued to remind Sarah that if she (Lara) goes down then Sarah's own income status would be considered to be wrong in some way or another, as she won it on a bet about the reality of human time-travelers being discovered. Well, in reality they haven't been discovered. Moreover, Lara told Sarah, "Everyone would wonder if you were in on the Psy-Op." That hit a nerve with Sarah, as she was not in on it, she was a victim, and yet she understood that people would debate that very point. Worse, Sarah thought, they would wrongly conclude that she was in on it. And Lara added "The press are largely leaving us in peace because I am a hero in the worlds view, and you are with me. BUT, if my reputation is in tatters then the press would no longer be considered the bad guys if they harassed us with reporters descending on our beautiful home. Indeed, they would be encouraged to harass us... hence they would do precisely that."

"F**k Lara. You are right but its like blackmail".

"Will you stop saying F**k!"

"No I f*****g will not stop saying F**k. This whole thing is F****d! But I cannot tell the world because I admit the undeniable fact that it would destroy me, you and I cannot make a decision as monumental as deciding whether it is best that humans are sedated and live a myth in order so they don't destroy themselves or whether it be best that they are free to decide with responsibility. Clearly you can make these f*****g monumental decisions. You think the human race be treated like little children. As for me, I do not feel like it should be me deciding humanity's future. Its like you are an ego maniac Lara. But I don't think that is quite true. I can see you are well-intentioned. I am just amazed you can think yourself worthy of making such a decision."

"So what happens now?"

"We live happily ever after" replied Sarah resulting in genuine (non-Oscar) tears welling up in Lara's eyes. She rushed over to Sarah, hugged her and they kissed.

Sarah had been unable to ruin her relationship and if you had prized open her brain to discover the slightest bias in terms of her monumental conflict she was experiencing, she would have just to say come down on Lara's side due to Sarah's great knowledge of the torture of Post Traumatic Stress Disorder which Sarah nicknamed 'Psychological Death'. However, Sarah's choice had profoundly negative consequences for the human race.

22 years later.

The remaining humans left on earth no longer believed Lara and Sarah, both of whom were in hiding. They would never be discovered by anyone as technology as we know it no longer existed so they were extremely difficult to track down, and detectives and investigative journalism no longer existed… so they were never questioned over their lies and to be honest, no one much cared as people were too traumatized over what nature had done to them. People had survival to think about. People who did mention Lara in conversation would predictably call her 'Lara the Liar'.

Because unfortunately if humanity were to ever recover from the multiple asteroid attack on earth that had wiped out 75% of the human race, then Lara would not be remembered as a hero. Indeed, she is lucky technology didn't exist as she wouldn't like what people would have said about her if they could of still accessed social media. You see, people hadn't believed the asteroids were going to hit earth. Everyone said that if they were to hit earth then Lara Hine would have told us about this as she is in contact with time travelers. Or of course, time travelers themselves would tell us. Thus there was a remarkable arrogance that the asteroids would somehow or other miss earth… or that the impact would be minimal. Sarah Aston tried to play the hero. She was going to tell the truth but Lara momentarily took her own wife hostage but almost instantly changed her mind and trusted that Sarah wouldn't do anything. She was right. Lara and Sarah were ultimately in this together.

In the aftermath of the disaster people reasoned that the time travel story must have been made up and thus what they had believed to be the nature of reality was in truth a new myth that had a relatively short shelf life. Lara of course was always well-intentioned but had she told the truth then more investment would have gone into defenses of all-kinds, including asteroid defenses, and the vast majority of people who died would have actually survived. Ironically Lara's lies hadn't saved lives, they had cost billions of lives. Sarah and Lara wrongly rationalized that all of this would have happened anyway. You could say, it was a good sedative, a good lie, a soothing myth that they told themselves.

In the Post-Apocalypse World UFO sightings (including very close-up sightings) increased by a staggering amount. In the Pre-Apocalypse World almost everyone would agree with the statement 'I have NOT recently seen a clear and close-up UFO." But in the Post Apocalypse World the vast majority would say they had recently seen a clear and close-up UFO. In this Post-Apocalypse World whatever controlled UFOs didn't care whether humans observed them or not. They did not make open contact but UFO's were much less stealthy. These things sure were very interested in what had happened to earth and its inhabitants.

As with everyone else, Lara and Sarah could never work out what the hell those UFOs were. Lara and Sarah could not explain the origins of the UFO intelligence that abducted people including frequently themselves.

THE END

Credits/Notes

·   This part of the book was slightly influenced by the scene and dialogue in the Netflix drama, Gypsy, episode 7 from about 30 – 38 minutes of the show.

"Take some of this shit. It's supposed to really get to what you might call 'the collective unconscious'. It opens up your mind".

"Geez Lara. I'm supposed to be more Freud than Jung. The only Jung book I have read is The Psychogenesis of Mental Disease. Jung was still kinda Freudian when he penned it".

"Sshhh. You know his theory though. And you are moving on right?"

"If having a more screwed up psyche means becoming more Jungian, then yes, I'm rather fundamentalist right now".

"Hhmmm, that's not an open mind Sarah. You naughty girl" said Lara while moving towards her girlfriend. "So are you going to take the DMT or are you going to take me?"

"Lara. You know me. Wine please. I like to maintain control."

"Control??? You are getting abducted by aliens against your will. Maybe the aliens will be more impressed with a Jungian Shaman than they would be a limiting Freudian".

Sarah takes hold of the pipe that Lara had dangling infront of her eyes and smokes it. About one second later Sarah is having a coughing fit.

"Ha Ha Ha. You know Sarah, that you get higher if you cough".

"I have messed up my mind. I might as well mess up my lungs".

"You are with me now. Your mind is cured."

"My first girlfriend at 37. I took my time."

"I know you slow coach. I'm only 36 and I'm there already".

Sarah goes sombre as she experiences a moment that Lue Elizondo expects people to experience when the real nature of reality hits them. She says

"How do you do it Lara? How do you stay so amazing following an alien abduction. You don't seem to be experiencing any PTSD symptoms whatsoever".

"In your language there's some Freudian repression and Jungian mask. But its mainly thanks to you. If I had experienced that on my own and if I were lonely I don't think I would cope as well. I also rationalize that the beings return us safely".

"I didn't see the truth" replies Sarah.

"And what is that exactly"?

"That we don't know what the truth is".

·   Credit to myself as none of this book was written by an AI writer.

·   People who are part of the UFO community will know exactly who the UFO researchers are that I referred to in this book. But for those who are unaware of some or all of the UFO researchers I mentioned, the following is for you. Ryan Robins twitter account is called Post Disclosure World. He is a real person and can be tweeted at the following address: @PostDisclosure His videos (in my opinion) are orientating and clarifying and he sometimes entertains with humor. Richard Dolan's twitter account is called Richard Dolan Intelligent Disclosure. His twitter account address is @I_D_Official In my book you read that Lara was about to purchase one of Dolan's books.

In real life Ross Coulthart is an Australian Journalist who has received intelligence from reliable and credible sources.Meanwhile Christopher Sharp is a British Journalist claiming that he has reliable and credible sources who he trusts. They have provided him with information concerning intact craft with Non Human Intelligence (NHI) origins. They are reversed engineered. I included a real life tweet of Christopher Sharp's in the fictional text.

Ross Coulthart's twitter account address is @RossCoulthart

Christopher Sharp's twitter account address is @ChrisUKSharp

Grant Cameron thinks consciousness is key to the UFO Phenomenon. As I wrote in the story, he refers to abductees who have used thought to control the UFO craft. His twitter account address is @GrantCameron

·   Halfway through the story Lara says "They play with reality like a toy". That is supposed to inform the reader that the ET's are also our world's simulators.

·   Where Sarah said "just remember the only thing that makes you interesting is me". That is almost a direct quote by Villanelle in Killing Eve. Villanelle words it "don't forget the only thing that makes you interesting is me". Killing Eve episode from Season 2. Episode title I Hope You Like Missionary.

·   Where Lara said "I think about you too. I mean I masturbate about you a lot". That is a direct quote by Villanelle in Killing Eve, Season 1. Episode title God I'm Tired.

·   The idea for Mike hiding under the bed listening to his ex wife making love to Lara is credited to the Netflix drama, 'YOU'. (See the Series 1, episode 6 episode titled Amour Fou… from 28:00 minutes to 29:30)

·   Leslie Kean is a real life reporter, albeit for the New York Times, not CNN. In my short story here, I wrote her as working for CNN reporting from New York City. In real life she is on of the UFO community's heroes as she, along with Helene Cooper and Ralph Blumenthal, broke the 2017 UFO story in the New York Times… it made the front cover and is credited with having made the UFO issue both more mainstream and also bringing more and more public figures out of the closet.

Two days after the 16 December 2017 Cooper/Blumenthal/Kean NYT report, Blumenthal wrote another NYT report based on the 16 December report. The 18 December article was titled On the Trail of a Secret Pentagon UFO Program. The opening paragraph hints at how big the UFO story could become. Blumenthal writes "Our readers are plenty interested in unidentified flying objects. We know that from the huge response to our front-page Sunday article (published online just after noon on Saturday) revealing a secret Pentagon program to investigate U.F.O.s. The piece, by the Pentagon correspondent Helene Cooper, the author Leslie Kean and myself — a contributor to The Times after a 45-year staff career — has dominated the most emailed and most viewed lists since".

·   Eric Weinstein is a cultural commentator and a podcast host. He has a PhD in Mathematical Physics attained at Harvard. He is credited with coining the term 'Intellectual dark Web'. He converted to thinking something big is going on concerning UFO's in 2022. He is interested in the deception and cover-up side of the issue. His twitter account address is @EricRWeinstein The pre-disclosure tweets that Lara highlighted are real quotes from Weinstein tweets from early May 2023.

·   Michael Masters is a Professor of Biological Anthropology. Author of Identified Flying Objects, The Extratempestrial Model, & Revelation. He supports the human time travel hypothesis as the answer to the origins of the intelligence behind the UFO craft. His twitter account address is @MorphoTime

I have no doubt about where my idea for Chapter 3 tile Lara: The Flawed Genius came from. Credit goes to the hugely successful Netflix drama called The Queens Gambit. In The Queens Gambit the main character, Beth Harmon plays the role of the flawed chess genius. The flawed genius is a familiar idea. Another successful drama that ran with this concept was House M.D. In House M.D. Hugh Laurie plays the role of the flawed medical genius, Gregory House.

Just like Beth ends up winning in The Queens Gambit, so too does Lara in Chapter 3.

In the Queens Gambit Beth is an alcoholic. The video below titled Every Cocktail featured in The Queens Gambit gets across her drinking habits very well… including the Gibson Martini which Lara Hine kept stashed away from Sarah's prying eyes. Then the video of Shocking Blue's Venus is included in these credits because (as you can see from the video below it) Beth Harmon's demons were (on one occasion) expressed while dancing, drinking, throwing up and collapsing to this song. And I include it as one of Lara's song choices.

https://youtu.be/pb6VB46ic9g

https://youtu.be/8LhkyyCvUHk

https://youtu.be/pSEnzwTOktU

No notes/credits required for Chapter 4.